# BILLIONAIRE BOSSHOLE

## A BEDDING THE BILLIONAIRE NOVEL

### LAURA LEE

Editor: Erin Potter
Proofreader: Ellie McLove of My Brother's Editor
Cover Design: Lori Jackson Design
Cover Model: Lucas Loyola
Photographer: Wander Aguiar Photography

# CHAPTER ONE

QUINN

"His dick must be *huge*."

I nearly sprayed my coffee all over the closing elevator doors. "Sylvie!"

"What?" My best friend shrugged. "If you think about it, statistically, he's packing some serious heat. You've seen his bulge. *Goddamn,* what I wouldn't give to be on the receiving end of that."

I pinched the bridge of my nose. I was going to need another triple latte to deal with her today. I loved Sylvie to death, but sometimes her lack of filter could be a bit much. Case in point: this discussion in a crammed elevator at eight o'clock on a Monday morning. I had no idea how our conversation had even taken this turn. One minute we were talking about getting drinks after work, and the next it was all dicks, all the time.

"Will you please stop talking about the man's penis?" I whisper-shouted.

She laughed. "Oh, c'mon, Quinn, you can't say you haven't thought about it. The man's a giant— what is he, like six-foot-three, six-foot-four? Easily two hundred ten pounds of drool-worthy muscle. I wonder how big of a baby he was. I'd bet my Chanel clutch that he's been obliterating vaginas since birth."

I groaned and mouthed an apology to the elderly woman standing beside me.

*Why is this damn thing so slow?*

I could not step off the elevator fast enough once we finally arrived on the fifty-first floor.

"Quinn!" Sylvie shouted, her ridiculous heels click-clacking on the marble floor. "Slow down!"

I sighed and waited for her to catch up. "You do realize there were at least a dozen other people trapped in that elevator with us, right?"

She scrunched her brows. "And?"

"Oh my God, you crazy woman, you can't just go around talking about the size of a man's cock. Especially not Ronan Maxwell's cock, *in his own damn building*! What if an employee heard us?"

Sylvie laughed. "First of all, if anyone has a problem talking about cock size, or cocks in general, they need to loosen up or get laid. Secondly, I never said the man's name." She looked around the reception area. "Although, *you* just did. Quite loudly, in fact."

I glanced around and sure enough, Antonio, the head receptionist, was snickering. Luckily for me, he was my other best friend.

I pointed at him. "Not a damn word."

He mimed buttoning his lips and batted his eyelashes. "My lips are sealed, honey. Although, if you're going to continue this conversation, you bitches better include me."

I glared at him. "Is he here yet?"

"Who?" Antonio asked innocently. "The owner of the cock in question?"

My eyes narrowed farther. "No, you idiot. The delivery guy from Stumptown."

"Oh, don't get your La Perlas in a bunch. He just left five minutes ago. Everyone will be sufficiently fed and caffeinated. Now, tell me more about Mr. Maxwell's D. The greater the detail, the better."

I growled, making both Antonio and Sylvie laugh, as I made my way down the long hallway leading to our main conference room.

Maxwell Hotels had recently acquired two gorgeous properties in Hawaii, and today we were meeting to discuss our new marketing campaign for the launch. When Sylvie and I got to the conference room, I immediately started rearranging the pastries so the muffins were on the left, the bagels were in the middle, and the Danishes were on the right. Our CEO, Ronan Maxwell, or as I liked to refer to him, the billionaire bosshole, was the most anally retentive person on the planet. I had no idea why, but the man had practically had an aneurysm the last time the pastries had been all mixed together. I had no desire to find yet another coffee vendor, so I was arranging them by height, just the way he preferred.

Sylvie switched on the projector, cueing up her PowerPoint presentation. She had been with the company for about four years as our creative director of marketing and I had been here just over two as Mr. Maxwell's executive assistant. Between you and me, she'd definitely gotten the better end of the deal. My salary might seem obscene to outsiders, but if they knew what I had to deal with on any given day, they'd think I was underpaid.

I walked to the front of the room and exchanged warm greetings with several members of our executive team as they filed in, taking their designated seats.

"Thank you for being here today. As you know, renovations for our new Hawaiian locations are near completion." I nodded to Sylvie. "Miss O'Hare's team has created a brilliant marketing campaign to capitalize on the upcoming high season. She's going to review each phase of—"

Mr. Maxwell then entered the room. As usual,

he was dressed impeccably in a charcoal designer suit—Prada, I was guessing—with a crisp white shirt. The overhead lights glinted off his signature platinum cufflinks as he looked at his watch.

His light blue eyes met mine and for a moment, I forgot about how much I loathed this man. His focus was so intense, it was a miracle I could finish my sentence. Ronan Maxwell was so beautiful, yet masculine, it took my breath away. Every inch of him was undeniably attractive, but my gaze always got hung up on his ridiculously full lips.

I couldn't tell you how many times I'd fantasized about tugging that lower lip between my teeth. If I didn't know better, I'd swear he got injections. As much as I'd like to deny it, my lady bits were instantly ready for action any time he was near. Hell, the man could practically make me come just with his deep, rumbly voice. It also didn't help that you could bounce a quarter off his ass and he always wore his dark brown hair in that freshly fucked way that I loved.

I looked away, deliberately ignoring how his perfectly tailored suit stretched across his broad chest. Once, I'd walked in on him changing, and I swear on my life, I almost orgasmed on the spot. Mr. Maxwell stood in the middle of his office, completely shirtless. For someone who worked so many hours, you wouldn't think his muscles would be so defined, but I could personally attest to the fact that they were. He even had that elusive V that turned smart women into dumbasses.

I had no idea when he fit time into his schedule for a workout, but I wouldn't lie and tell you that I wasn't grateful. It was only a matter of seconds before he pulled on a new shirt—one that didn't have a giant coffee stain on it—but that brief moment in time had inspired more than one X-rated dream. If nothing else, the man was good for that.

"We all know why we're here," Head Asshole barked. "Now, since you make a *much* better door than a window, if you'll move aside so we can actually *see* the slides, that'd be fantastic, Miss Montgomery."

*Well, that certainly reminds me how much of a jerk he is.*

I took the seat closest to Sylvie and gestured for her to begin her presentation. I was only half-listening since I'd already seen all the slides, which was probably a good thing since Mr. Maxwell was being his usual condescending self. Sylvie fielded his questions like the marketing badass that she was, and when she reached the end of her PowerPoint, the other executives were looking at her with admiration, clearly pleased with her presentation.

Mr. Maxwell, of course, was never satisfied with anything. "Miss O'Hare, is this truly the best idea your team could come up with?" He gestured to the projector screen. "Surely, you can think of a more original slogan than 'A Taste of Paradise in Paradise.'"

Sylvie cleared her throat. "Mr. Maxwell, as I mentioned in my presentation, that slogan is what our panel of testers responded best to."

He rolled his eyes. "I don't give a *shit* what testers responded best to. I care about what's going to max out our occupancy. What's going to boost sales for spa services and guest excursions. I care about what's going to *make me and our share-holders money*. And this slogan is *not* it. Understand?"

She blinked rapidly. "Yes, sir. We'll come up with more ideas and get those to you by the end of the week."

"You have until Thursday, or you'll all be looking for new jobs. Am I clear?" Mr. Maxwell folded his arms over his chest.

Sylvie nodded and began closing down her laptop. "Yes, sir."

Mr. Maxwell looked around the room. "Well, what are you waiting for? The meeting is over. Get out of here."

*Ugh, he is such an ass.*

As I headed toward the door, Mr. Maxwell said, "Not you, Miss Montgomery. I'd like a word."

Sylvie mouthed *good luck* as she stepped out of the room.

I mirrored his stance and crossed my arms. "Yes?"

He stared at me without a word. When he licked his bottom lip, unbidden images of him tracing that tongue over my skin flashed before me. What was wrong with me? This man was the biggest jerk I'd ever met, yet I couldn't stop fantasizing about him in every compromising situation imaginable.

"You approved Miss O'Hare's presentation?"

I lifted my chin. "Yes, I did, because it was a damn good one."

He scoffed. "Funny, I thought you would've learned by now that I *do not* accept mediocrity. Those ideas were 'damn good' if we were a budget hotel chain. Need I remind you that we are one of the largest *luxury* hotel chains in the world, Miss Montgomery?"

My eyes narrowed. "I am *well* aware, Mr. Maxwell."

"Could've fooled me."

I had to literally bite my tongue to avoid an outburst. "Will there be anything else?" The *fuck off* was implied in my tone.

When he stood, my eyes automatically fell to the bulge Sylvie had mentioned. Holy hell, was he getting hard?

"My eyes are up here, Miss Montgomery."

*Shit!*

I could feel my cheeks flushing, but I brushed it off, like I wasn't just caught staring at his crotch. "I'm also well aware of that."

The asshole smirked. "Of course you are. You're dismissed. Get the hell out of my conference room."

I brushed past him, refusing to acknowledge what that cocky smile did to me.

"Oh, and Miss Montgomery?"

I paused over the threshold and looked over my shoulder. "Yes?"

"Next time you waste my time by approving a shit campaign like that, you'll be looking for a new job, too."

Like I said. Ass. Hole.

# CHAPTER TWO

**RONAN**

"Do you think he goes downtown? Fuck, what I wouldn't give to have that man's head between my thighs."

My EA chuckled at her friend, Miss O'Hare. "Yeah, right. Ronan Maxwell wouldn't eat pussy unless it increased his net worth. Nothing about that man indicates that he's a giver."

*Ah, Miss Montgomery, how wrong you are. I'd be more than happy to show you how much I love eating pussy.*

"That's too bad," Miss O'Hare mused.

"Agreed," Miss Montgomery said. "I can't tell you how many nights I've gotten off to fantasies of him going down on me. Just this morning, I woke up so damn wet from dreaming about him that I had to Jill off in the shower three times."

*Well, this conversation just got a lot more interesting.*

For the last fifteen minutes, I'd been listening in on them. My lunch meeting had been canceled at the last minute, so Miss Montgomery had no idea I was still in the building. I was just about to step out to grab a bite when I heard the ladies returning with their takeout. I wasn't sure what had stopped me, but when their voices rang through the slight crack in the doorway, curiosity got the best of me. Now, I was on the couch that sat against our shared wall, trying not to breathe too loudly.

"I'm telling you, Quinn, I think you should go for it. Just walk into his office, take that big dick out of his pants, and give him the ride of his life. I'd bet you anything that he'd be much nicer to you after that."

Miss Montgomery laughed. "Yeah, right. That prick is incapable of being nice. And I'm still not convinced on your theory about the size of his cock. His special brand of assholery tells me that he's compensating for something. Plus, he drives a McLaren. I mean, c'mon, if that doesn't scream tiny dick, I don't know what does."

*I'd be more than happy to prove you wrong, sweetheart.*

Fuck, said cock was getting painfully hard just thinking about it. I pressed my open palm against my fly, willing it to calm down. I'd known Quinn Montgomery would be trouble the moment I'd laid eyes on her. Human Resources handled all of the hiring around here, so I hadn't met her until her first day on the job. When I'd caught sight of her long blonde hair, those bee-stung lips, and luscious curves, I'd instantly wanted to push her up against the wall and fuck her senseless.

The first year that she worked here, I'd bedded several hot blondes, trying to squash my attraction to her. Unfortunately for me—and my dick—I was always left wanting in the end. So much so, that I'd stopped trying. Over the last twelve months, I'd had nothing but my hand and fantasies of my sexy-as-fuck assistant. To say that I was sexually frustrated would be a massive understatement.

The most aggravating part—besides the fact that she worked for me so I couldn't go there—was that I knew she wanted me, too. I didn't need to eavesdrop on this conversation to confirm that. I saw the longing looks she gave me when she thought I wasn't watching. How often her eyes hungrily roamed my body. Hell, she was staring at my crotch like she wanted to swallow my dick just a few hours ago. When she gave me that look, it took every ounce of willpower that I possessed not to pin her to the conference table. The woman couldn't stand me, no doubt, but she fucking *wanted* me.

My ears perked up when I heard Miss Montgomery speaking again. "This fixation of mine is getting ridiculous, Syl. Why can't I get him out of my head?"

"You know what I think?" Miss O'Hare replied through what I assumed was a mouthful of food.

"What?"

"You need to get laid. The last time was that cute guy from accounting, right?"

*Which* guy from accounting?

Miss Montgomery groaned. "Yeah. Over *a year* ago. And that was underwhelming at best. The only reason I even got off was because I took matters into my own hand and started fantasizing about my stupid boss."

"Ah, he does make great material," Miss O'Hare laughed. "What about L.A. Singles?"

"The dating app?" Miss Montgomery questioned. "I don't know if online dating is really the right thing for me."

"Why not? It's perfect for someone like you."

I could almost see Miss Montgomery's brows pinching together. "What's that supposed to mean?"

"Oh, calm down, Quinn. I was referring to how many hours you work. Online dating is pretty much the only way for busy professionals to meet someone outside of the workplace anymore. The only reason not to do it would be if you had your sights set on someone here."

"I don't know..." Miss Montgomery hedged.

"What harm would it do? Just download the app so you can at least browse the guys. You don't need to make your profile public until you're ready."

Miss Montgomery sighed. "Okay, fine. It's downloading."

Her friend clapped. "We're gonna get you laid by the weekend!"

"I didn't say I was going to contact anyone!"

Miss O'Hare scoffed. "Sure you will. As beautiful as he is, masturbating to your boss cannot be your sole source of action. You need a real dick before the cobwebs set in. Now, what do you want your profile name to be?"

"Is it really that important?"

"Of course it is!" her friend insisted. "You need something intriguing. Something that suits you."

There was a moment of silence before Miss Montgomery spoke. I could imagine her sexy little smile as she said, "What about Egomaniacs-Need-Not-Apply?"

Miss O'Hare snorted. "Oh my God, that's perfect!"

"Right? I only have room for one massively self-absorbed person in my life and that guy pays me a shit-ton of money to put up with him. I'm sure as hell not going to spend time with someone like that for free."

Both women laughed. I, however, hadn't found her comment nearly as funny.

"As fun as this is, I've gotta get back so I can think of some more slogans," Miss O'Hare said.

"God, he's such an ass. That slogan is perfect."

"Meh, I'm used to it by now. When has he ever accepted anything on the first try?"

"True," Miss Montgomery agreed. "You wanna head downstairs with me to load up on caffeine first?"

"Sure. I have a feeling I'm going to need it."

I waited until I was sure they were gone before exiting my office. Before I could think better of it, I winked at Miss Montgomery's double take as I passed the coffee cart on my way out of the building. I wasn't about to show my cards, but what was the harm in letting her sweat it out? If nothing else, it would teach her to guard her personal conversations more carefully while in the office.

# CHAPTER THREE

## QUINN

If he didn't pay me so much, I swear I would've quit on my first day. Okay, that was a lie; I worked damn hard to get this position and I intended to keep it for as long as it suited my goals. He may have been an insufferable asshole, but Ronan Maxwell was a brilliant businessman. You didn't become the CEO of a multi-billion-dollar corporation if you weren't. Sure, he inherited the role from his father, but he'd deserved it. In fact, I think *because* this was his family's legacy, he worked even harder to prove himself.

Not that he'd admit that. The bastard was far too cocky.

Before me, Mr. Maxwell had a revolving door

of EAs. No one lasted more than a few months because they couldn't handle the stress. The man had ridiculously high standards, but he practiced what he preached, so I couldn't really fault him for it. It was his delivery of those expectations that made me want to backhand him more often than not.

Besides, I was too stubborn to give up. My mother always told me that I was the most pigheaded person she'd ever met. Little did she know at the time how valuable that particular trait would become. I'd learned so much from Ronan Maxwell over the last two years—things I didn't need to know for my current position, but he'd taken the time to teach me anyway.

Hospitality was never on my radar before because I was a numbers geek through and through, but now that I better understood the scope of it, I loved it. Putting up with my asshole boss gave me the best chance of success in this field.

"Nice of you to finally show up. I thought at this point you had taken the rest of the day off." I looked up, startled by the deep voice. Mr. Maxwell was standing in the doorway to my office that served as the antechamber to his.

"Of course not, Mr. Maxwell." My voice was sugary sweet but laced with arsenic. "I would never dream of doing such a thing without permission."

He folded his arms and leveled me with a glare.

"What took you so damn long?"

I resisted the urge to roll my eyes. "This is Los Angeles, sir. Traffic at any time of day is a nightmare. Since you decided to send me across town in the middle of the evening rush hour on a Friday, it was even worse. My apologies for not having the ability to steamroll over thousands of vehicles so I could return sooner."

I'd swear he was stifling a laugh. "I want the final travel itinerary for Hawaii on my desk by seven. And order some food from Emperor's Dragon. I'll have the Chicken Manchurian with a side of barbeque pork. Get something for yourself, too. We have a lot more to cover before the day is through." With that, he spun on his heels, slamming his office door behind him.

Ugh, I didn't know what had crawled up his ass, but he'd been even worse than usual this week. I'd gone home no earlier than nine o'clock every evening. I foolishly thought that since it was Friday, he'd let me go at a reasonable hour. Instead, while everyone else was heading home for the weekend, I was stuck here with the biggest dick on the planet. Knowing him, I'd be lucky to get out of here before midnight.

"Mr. Maxwell, did you hear what I said?"

He blinked rapidly. "No."

What was wrong with him? He was the most observant man I knew. He was normally ten steps ahead of everyone else, in every situation. Tonight, he was abnormally quiet and staring off into space a lot. It was freaking me out.

"I said, I really don't think we should charge our guests for the luau. They're paying at least five hundred dollars per night, which easily covers the expense. It should be a perk, like free continental breakfast."

"Miss Montgomery, correct me if I'm wrong, but you are rather a *savant* with numbers, correct?" Mr. Maxwell said, as if he thought I was adorably naïve. "And a Stanford graduate?"

I gritted my teeth. "Were those rhetorical questions?"

He raised an absurdly sexy eyebrow. "Why would I waste my breath uttering rhetorical questions?"

"Because we both know you already know the answer to both of those questions." I narrowed my eyes for emphasis.

The bastard smirked as he stood up and rounded his desk. "Indulge me, if you will."

I sighed. "Yes, I am rather proficient with financial analysis and both my bachelor's *and* MBA are from Stanford."

He leaned against the edge of the mahogany

and crossed his arms over his chest. "So, as an Ivy League graduate, one could assume you were familiar with the concept that higher profits for any business was a good thing, correct?"

White-hot visions of jamming my spikey shoe into his shin ran through my head.

"Yes. Your point being?"

"My *point* is that our target clientele can easily afford to pay admission to a luau. Why wouldn't we want to increase our profits by charging them for it? Especially for one of this caliber? Plus, when have we *ever* offered a free meal service?"

I was clenching my jaw so hard, I swore I was about to do permanent damage. I didn't like the fact that he was looming over me so I rose from my chair and mimicked his posture. "Never."

"Exactly. Now, tell me, Miss Montgomery, what type of hotel chain *does* offer free continental breakfasts?"

My body stiffened as I realized I was on the losing end of this debate. "Budget hotel chains."

He flashed a self-righteous grin. "Right again. And what type of hotel chain are we?"

I had to consciously fight the desire to curl my fists. "We are a luxury hotel chain, sir. As you already know."

"Of course, *I* know." He undid his cufflinks and rolled his sleeves up. "But it seems like *you* need constant reminders lately."

"I can assure you that I do *not*."

I could feel my face flushing in anger and there wasn't a damn thing I could do about it. Once I was this riled up, it was almost impossible to conceal my emotions. I was normally an expert at keeping my cool when Mr. Maxwell pushed my buttons, but insulting my intelligence was the exception to that, it seemed. It was a line he had never crossed before, so I was a bit off-kilter.

He laughed mockingly. "Could've fooled me."

Okay, that was the last straw. I had officially reached my limit. "You're an asshole."

Holy shit! I couldn't believe I'd just said that out loud.

Mr. Maxwell's ears reddened as he took a few steps toward me. "*What* did you say, Miss Montgomery?"

I propped a hand on my hip. "You heard me."

He took one more step and gripped the edge of the desk on each side of me, effectively caging me in. "Let's say I didn't. Go ahead and repeat what you said. *I fucking dare you.*"

Well, crap, there was no sense in backing down now. My pride wouldn't allow it. I tilted my chin up and looked him directly in the eyes. "I said, *you're an asshole*. Surely that's not the first time someone's called you that."

The look he gave me as he rolled my words around in his head was sinful. Predatory, even. I

21

could feel the flood of arousal in my panties, but I remained aloof on the surface. It was probably only a handful of seconds, but it felt like an eternity as we engaged in a silent showdown. I didn't know which one of us lunged first, but before I knew it, our lips were pressed against each other's.

I gasped when I felt his hand on my hip, which he took as an open invitation to invade my mouth with his tongue. After that, all hope of pretending this wasn't happening was gone. Damn, Ronan Maxwell knew how to own a woman's mouth. I'd imagined kissing him hundreds of times—maybe even thousands—but nothing could've prepared me for the reality. He teased me with his tongue, nibbled on my lips, commanded every move. He kissed like he did everything—with pure alpha male dominance. I had never been as willing to submit to someone's will as I was now. As our mouths moved against each other's, his thumb inched perilously close to my ass. Fingers clenched around the stretchy fabric of my skirt, as if he were resisting the urge to rip it off my body.

*God, I wanted him to rip it off of my body.*

I didn't think I had ever wanted to mount someone and ride them off into the sunset as badly as I did now. A million thoughts raced through my head at once. What was he thinking? Did he feel the same jolt of electricity running through his veins? Why, after two years, did he decide to touch me?

From the moment we met, this man had gone out of his way to avoid physical contact. This—whatever it was—was undoubtedly intentional. And as much as I hated to admit it, incredibly arousing.

Mr. Maxwell's hand wandered down the side of my thigh to the hem of my skirt. When his thumb glided from side to side over the back of my leg, shivers raced down my spine.

"What's going on in that head of yours?" his deep voice rumbled.

"So many things," I whispered.

His hand climbed higher, dangerously close to discovering how wet my panties were. "Would you like me to stop?"

My brain was screaming, *Yes! Run out of the room, dumbass!* while my head was shaking emphatically.

"I need the words, Miss Montgomery."

My heart was pounding in my chest. I knew this was crazy. I knew this was stupid. But I couldn't tell him to stop if my life had depended on it. "Don't stop."

Mr. Maxwell released a harsh exhale. "Thank fuck."

When I met his gaze, his blue eyes were filled with questions, with unrestrained *desire*. I couldn't sort out how I felt about that. I'd spent the last two years fantasizing about this man. Sure, some of those fantasies involved throwing my Jimmy Choos at his forehead, but mostly, they were sexual in nature. *Deeply* sexual in nature. Frankly, I wasn't entirely sure this wasn't a dream.

But then I remembered that my dreams never felt this real. I had never felt the warmth of his touch. Never smelled the spiciness of his cologne. Never heard my pulse pounding in my ears. No, this was very much happening, and I was an all-too-willing participant. Lord help me, but I was *so* on board with this plan, no matter how fucked up it was.

Mr. Maxwell leaned into my body, causing me to bend slightly backward to maintain eye contact. Even wearing five-inch heels, the man still towered over me. Damn, he really was a giant. It was even more apparent standing so close to him.

I braced my hands on the edge of his desk when he reached out with two fingers and traced the length of my jaw. He continued down the slope of my neck and across the width of my collarbone. When he feathered them against the side of my breast, I moaned, making his sexy lips curl up in the corners. With both hands now resting at the curve of my waist, Mr. Maxwell lifted me onto the wooden surface, causing my skirt to ride up my thighs.

We both watched as he bunched the material in his hands, slowly pushing it toward my waist until my satin blue panties were revealed. My body was on autopilot, parting my legs without question, allowing him to look his fill. His breathing quickened and his eyes sparkled when he noticed the obvious wet spot.

I bit my lip when he ran the pad of his thumb over the dampness. "Is this for me, Miss Montgomery? Is your pussy aching, begging for my mouth? My cock?"

"You'd like that, wouldn't you?" I whimpered when he slipped beneath the fabric and ran his finger down my slit.

He gave me a wolfish grin. "Oh, I'd like that *very much* and I suspect you would, too."

"God," I panted as he pushed one long finger inside me. I moaned shamelessly when he added another.

He closed his eyes as he pumped in and out, but I couldn't tear my eyes away. From the sheer ecstasy on his face. From the fingers gliding in and out of my body. From the muscles bunching beneath his shirt. I was memorizing every minute detail in that moment, reveling in how incredible it felt.

I must've been losing my mind, I'd decided. There was no other explanation for why I was more turned on than I'd ever been in my life. How did we even get to this point, I wondered? Two minutes ago, we were talking about luaus, and now, my boss was finger fucking me on his desk.

Mr. Maxwell's eyes snapped open. "Fuck. You're so tight. So goddamn wet. If I had known you'd be this responsive, I would've done this a helluva lot sooner."

"Stop talking," I whined.

He released a throaty chuckle. "Make me."

I narrowed my eyes at him. "Bastard."

He winked. "Never claimed not to be."

I growled in frustration. Fine, if he wouldn't shut up, I would *make him* shut up. I grabbed his silver tie and yanked him down to my mouth. When he wouldn't cooperate, I sucked on his pillowy lower lip.

"Kiss me, goddammit."

He smiled against my lips. "So bossy."

I bit him this time, and he finally caved. Our kisses were not gentle. They were an erotic duel of sucking, licking, and biting. Mr. Maxwell continued fucking me with his fingers while rolling the pad of his thumb over my clit. He worked me over so well, my body had no choice but to climb higher and higher until I was freefalling into an abyss.

When my inner muscles stopped clenching, he withdrew his fingers and pressed them against my lips, prompting me to open. I sucked them into my mouth down to the knuckle, locking eyes with him the entire time. God, this was such a lewd act, but it was also so erotic, I couldn't find the will to care. And with the way Mr. Maxwell was looking at me, I'd say he was just as turned on by it as I was.

When he withdrew his fingers, I made quick

work of his belt buckle and unzipped his slacks. My hand dove into his boxer briefs and grabbed onto his cock. Jesus, he was huge! Sylvie was right; the man was packing some serious heat.

Mr. Maxwell groaned as I stroked his length.

"Do you even know how to use this thing?"

He gave me a wicked grin. "I'm going to make you regret that, wiseass."

I raised an eyebrow in challenge. "Go ahead. Put your money where your mouth is. Or in this case, your dick."

He retrieved a condom from his wallet and shoved my hand away to slide it down his shaft. Once he was fully sheathed, he moved my panties to the side and pressed the flared head against my entrance. "Last chance to back out, Miss Montgomery."

I scoffed. "Not happening. Show me what you've got."

He made a low, growly noise as he untucked my blouse and ripped it over my head. His hands slid up my ribcage, to my breasts, until he was moving his thumbs over my erect nipples through my bra. The combination of his rough touch and the lacy fabric was almost too much. I was on stimulation overload, yet I still couldn't get enough. I pressed into his palms, demanding more.

Losing patience, I leaned back on my elbows, dug my heels into his ass and pulled him forward.

Mr. Maxwell took the hint and in one smooth motion, thrust deep inside of me. My moans echoed throughout the room, which should've been appalling to me, but it wasn't, because he felt too good. Better than any man I'd ever been with. He instantly made me wild with lust. I screamed, I cursed, I shamelessly begged for more.

He leaned over, fanning his arms to clear the surface, and set a punishing rhythm. I was vaguely aware of various desk items hitting the floor, but that was drowned out by the sound of our skin slapping together.

"What's that, Miss Montgomery? You want more?" His jaw clenched as he went deeper, harder. "It sure seems like I *do* know how to use this thing, doesn't it? You've never had better dick."

Oh my God, why did I suddenly find his cockiness unbearably hot? He laughed mockingly when my eyes rolled back as he thumbed my clit.

"Mediocre at best," I lied.

Mr. Maxwell grabbed my ankle and propped my stiletto over his shoulder. Fuck, he was so deep like this, I knew I would be sore later. To my absolute horror, I found myself pleased with that fact.

"Such a fucking liar," he seethed. "Your pussy is dripping all over my cock. You've *never* been fucked this thoroughly before."

There was no way in hell I was telling him that he was right. "Shut. Up."

"Or what?" he taunted as he yanked my bra cup down and pinched my nipple.

"Ahhh... God... just stop talking and make me come!"

He gave me a wicked smile. "Say please, Miss Montgomery."

My eyes flew to his and narrowed. "Fuck. You."

He pushed in even harder. "Already doing that, sweetheart." He circled my nub until I was on the precipice of release. Right before I flew over, he pulled his thumb away.

"Fuck!" I balled my fists and screamed in frustration. "Do you always have to be such a bastard? Think about someone other than yourself for a change!"

"Say..." Thrust. "Please." Thrust.

I tried to take matters into my own hands, but he cuffed my wrists over my head before I could do so. "Motherfu—"

He stilled inside of me and bit my lip so hard, I was sure he'd drawn blood. "Nice try. Now, why don't you be a good girl and ask nicely?" When I refused to speak, he started toying with my slick flesh again, until I was a writhing, whimpering mess. "Say please and I'll make you come so hard you'll forget why you were mad at me."

I tried to resist. I really did. But when he started moving again, driving himself deeper and harder with each thrust, all while moving his thumb against my clit using the perfect amount of pressure, I couldn't take it anymore.

I groaned. "Please!"

He turned his head and bit the skin right above my ankle. "Please, *what?*"

I glared. "Please make me come, you fucking bastard!"

Mr. Maxwell smiled down at me. "It'll be my pleasure, Miss Montgomery."

Within seconds, lightning shot down my spine and I was screaming. Quaking. Gasping for air. When my orgasm finally subsided, he bent forward and began moving with renewed purpose. I knew his biting kisses down my neck would leave marks, but in that moment, I didn't care. I wanted whatever he would give me. I wanted every part of him.

He wasn't the asshole who'd been tormenting me for the last two years. He wasn't even my boss. He was simply a beautiful man who was responsible for the best sexual experience of my life. My fantasies, as plentiful as they were, hadn't done him justice. If sex were an Olympic sport, Ronan Maxwell would take home the gold every damn time, leaving a heap of quivering women in his wake.

With one final thrust, he buried his face into my neck and found his own release. After a few moments, he placed one surprisingly gentle kiss on my neck, pulled out of me, and took a step back.

Suddenly feeling awkward, I hopped off the desk, pulling my skirt down my thighs. I couldn't bring myself to look at him now that I was no longer blinded by lust. Regret and shame hung heavily in the air. I spotted my blouse on the floor, picked it up, and quickly pulled it over my head. The seconds ticked by in silence, the only sounds in the room were the pull of a zipper, the clang of a belt buckle, and the swishing of fabric as we dressed.

When I had finally made myself presentable, I hurried out of his office, praying that my shaky legs wouldn't betray me. I retrieved my purse from my desk, not even bothering to check if I had shut down my computer, and bolted to the elevators.

"Come on, come on," I whispered, as I bounced frantically, waiting for the lift to arrive.

Once it did, I ran inside and pressed the button for the underground garage. As the doors were closing, I made the mistake of looking up. Mr. Maxwell was standing no more than five feet away, looking at me with pure hatred in his gaze. He made no attempt to stop me, he just stood there, staring me directly in the eyes, so I could feel the full force of his rage.

Five minutes ago, this man had made me feel better than I would've ever thought possible. Now, I didn't think I could possibly feel any worse.

*What had I done?*

# CHAPTER FOUR

**RONAN**

I was so fucked.

As I watched Miss Montgomery flee, all I could think about was how incredible her pussy felt. How perfectly we fit together. Over the last two years, I'd pictured it countless times, but my fantasies could never capture the sheer ecstasy of being inside that woman. Of seeing her writhe beneath me, begging me for more.

I thrived on control. The fact that she'd made me lose it made me furious. I couldn't stop thinking about the conversation I'd overheard on Monday. It was becoming a distraction—practically to the point of obsession. In fact, I'd been adding an excessive amount of work to Miss Montgomery's plate all week just so I could have more time with her.

Plus, if I was being completely honest with myself, I couldn't stand the thought of her meeting someone online. Even worse, fucking them as she was likely thinking of me. I was ashamed to admit this, but I downloaded that dating app on my phone, and I'd been keeping an eye out for her profile. She hadn't gone live with it yet, but that didn't mean she wouldn't eventually.

When Miss Montgomery had called me an asshole, I'd snapped. That's the only explanation for what happened. The tempting curve of her breasts so close, taunting me. My fingers twitched, dying to wrap her thick waves of hair around my fist. Her vanilla fragrance was so inviting, I needed to know if she tasted as sweet as she smelled. I wanted more than anything to feel her tremble beneath me.

As my hand wrapped around her hip, quite frankly, I was expecting a solid knee to the balls. But when she inhaled sharply and leaned into my touch, I was done for. And as I finally sunk into her warm, tight body, I was so blissed out, she had absolute power over me. In that moment, I would've given her anything. Done anything. That woman fucking *owned* me.

And I fucking hated her for it.

I scrubbed a hand over my face and headed back into my office. The moment I stepped inside, I knew what a mistake that had been. The room reeked like sex. Papers and cartons of Chinese food littered the floor. The evidence of our tryst was staring me in the face, mocking me. But as pissed as I was, sadly, my dick didn't hate the reminder. He jerked at the sight.

*Fucking traitor.*

As I was picking up the mess, something shiny caught my eye. Upon closer inspection, I saw it was a diamond earring. Miss Montgomery's diamond earring to be exact. It was a simple stud, and not very large considering her salary, but she wore these things every single day. I often wondered if they had some sort of sentimental value. Then I reminded myself that I didn't give a shit what accessories she wore as long as she looked professional.

Maybe if I kept telling myself that, I'd believe it.

I didn't know what to expect the following Monday. Any person in my position would've probably been waiting for the sexual harassment charges to hit. With the whole *#MeToo* movement, it was certainly a possibility. The world finally gave a shit about women's treatment in the workplace, and sometimes, it was taken to the extreme.

Don't get me wrong; I fully supported the cause. I donated a considerable amount of money to it, in fact. There were plenty of men out there who couldn't take a hint and *no* woman should be subjected to that. That said, there were also plenty of women in the world who liked to create drama where there was none, and this was their perfect opportunity. If you didn't believe that to be true, you were a moron.

But for some reason, I didn't think Miss Montgomery was one of those women. She was young—almost ten years my junior—but she was a consummate professional. Loyal. Genuinely dedicated to her position. From her first day on the job, she took the initiative to learn about what it took to run a successful hotel chain, even in areas outside of her job description. She had completed every single task without hesitation or complaint and God knows I'd given her more than a few reasons to complain.

Miss Montgomery was one of the rare millennials who didn't have some misguided sense of entitlement. Most thought they deserved the world simply because they woke up that morning, but not her. She truly understood that you needed to work hard to succeed. You needed to prove yourself, that it took time to earn a promotion. She knew that you needed to act for the position you *wanted*, not the position you had. Most of the dipshits we hired fresh out of college never lasted more than a few months because they didn't share her outlook. It was one of the many traits that made her extraordinary.

Too bad she was also a wretched bitch.

I swear, that woman knew how to antagonize me like no other. She was always mindful, never quite crossing the line into insubordinate—well, until last Friday anyway—but she had fire. She was the only person in this building who didn't take my shit when I was being an outright bastard—which, let's face it, was more often than not. I respected the hell out of her for it, but it also annoyed the fuck out of me. Mostly because it made my dick hard.

Speaking of... Miss Montgomery had just arrived. This early in the day, the constant hum around an office this size was almost nonexistent, so I could hear the subtle creak as she opened the door to her office, which was the interior to mine. The clank of keys hitting the surface of her desk. I imagined her hanging her coat on the rack as I'd seen her do hundreds of times in the past right before she sat down and powered up her computer.

I wondered what she was wearing today. Would she torture me with one of those tight skirts and sky-high shoes that she favored? Her clothing was never provocative, but the way the fabric hugged her curves, kept me in a perpetual state of arousal. She seemed to have an endless supply of red too, which happened to be my favorite color.

Christ, what was wrong with me? I couldn't stand the woman, yet my dick refused to listen. Here I was, daydreaming about women's fashion, for fuck's sake. I had an empire to run—the last thing I should've been doing was thinking about someone who drove me crazy.

I pulled up my calendar to check my schedule for the day and swore when I saw the first appointment on my agenda. Miss Montgomery and I were scheduled to meet with my finance team to review the third quarter budget projections. It wasn't something she *needed* to sit in on, but as soon as I figured out how brilliant she was with figures, the entrepreneur in me couldn't resist.

She had become so keen on dissecting each line item, suggesting effective ways to cut costs that even my CFO missed, I relied on her input. It was a win-win situation: I was able to increase my profit margin and she got on-the-job experience to add to her resume.

I wasn't an idiot; I knew she wouldn't be my assistant forever. She's far too intelligent and driven. But if I had my way, she would stay with my company. I was a firm believer in growing talent from within, and one thing Miss Montgomery had in spades, was talent.

In more ways than one, as I'd recently learned.

I just hoped that what had happened between us Friday night didn't fuck things up. Why did the sex have to be so goddamn phenomenal? I always thought that if one day, my fantasies came to fruition, the real thing would never measure up and I'd be able to move on.

Now, I had firsthand knowledge of what she looked like nearly naked. The sound that she made when she came. Shit, I even felt regret, not having had the opportunity to taste her pussy. I jerked off countless times over the weekend imagining what it would be like.

Not only was I still thinking about her in every pornographic way possible, but it was now amplified because I knew how great it could be. So much for getting over my attraction to her.

Fuck.

I rubbed a hand over my mouth, mentally preparing myself for what was about to happen. The only way to find out what kind of aftermath I was dealing with was to face the problem head-on.

# CHAPTER FIVE

QUINN

What a shit morning.

I'd only been in the office for five minutes, yet I was mentally ready to call it a day. On top of the fact that I'd had maybe two hours' worth of sleep, traffic on the way in was even more horrific than usual. Then, when I finally pulled off the 10, some idiot cut me off, clipping the front panel of my brand-new Audi in the process. After exchanging insurance information with him, the heel of my favorite Valentino pumps broke off as I was walking back to my car. Thankfully, I always had a spare pair of shoes in my trunk, but of course, they were my least favorite.

The icing on the shitastic cake was that one of my grandmother's diamond earrings had gone missing. They were a family heirloom, and one of my most prized possessions. I'd worn them every day for the last five years, yet sometime on Friday, one fell out, and I had yet to find it. I'd never needed those damn earrings more than I did right now.

I wanted to look my absolute best today. I needed the extra confidence to pull this off, yet fate seemed to be conspiring against me. After debating all weekend, I decided late last night that I would forget the whole *incident* with Mr. Maxwell ever happened. There was no way I was going to let a weak moment on my part doom my career. Nor was I going to give that bastard the satisfaction of knowing I wanted more.

*God, I wanted more.*

But that would never happen, I reminded myself. It was a one-time only event. A colossal mistake. One that I will *never* repeat, under any circumstances. If Mr. Maxwell happened to bring it up, I was just going to deny, deny, deny. He was a smart man; he'd catch on quickly. So what if I couldn't stop thinking about how great he felt? How long and thick his cock was. How I'd never had orgasms as powerful as the two that he gave me.

Nope.

I was going to purge the whole thing from my memory and move on. I was so determined to do just that, that I changed my privacy setting and threw myself into the online dating world. I wouldn't settle for just anyone, but I *would* dive into the sea of single Los Angelenos.

There were plenty of men out there who were equally as gorgeous as Mr. Maxwell. Plus, they weren't my boss, so really, *anyone* else would be a better choice. Not that I'd ever consider dating Mr. Maxwell, mind you. Purely the thought of that was laughable. I knew he had no problem attracting a woman. I just couldn't imagine him being nice to anyone long enough to make them want to stick around.

I took a deep breath and straightened my spine as he opened the door to his office. I didn't know what approach he'd go with, but whichever he chose, I was going to make damn sure I took control of the situation.

"Miss Montgomery," he said by way of greeting.

His eyes widened and then narrowed into slits when he saw what I was wearing. I smiled to myself at his reaction. I knew he loved this dress on me. I always caught him staring at my ass when I wore it. I didn't wear it for him though—it just happened to be the only work-appropriate piece in my closet that I could pair with my favorite infinity scarf. A scarf that was absolutely necessary thanks to him. My hair could only do so much in hiding the fading bruises his mouth had left behind. Who did that douchebag think he was anyway, leaving hickeys all over me like a horny teenager?

I returned his glare. "Good morning, Mr. Maxwell."

He raised an eyebrow. "Is it? A good morning?"

*Deny. Deny. Deny.*

"Of course. Why wouldn't it be?"

Mr. Maxwell scratched the light stubble over his jaw, not saying a word. He stared at me so intently, carefully cataloging each of my features. I knew what he was doing; he was trying to determine my next move so he could best me. Too bad for him, I wasn't going to let that happen.

I averted my gaze to my computer screen. "Your first meeting is in fifteen. After that, you have a conference call with the London office. Would you like me to get you a mocha from downstairs beforehand or will the drip coffee in the conference room be suitable to your refined palette?"

His jaw ticked. "Refined palette?"

I stood up and crossed my arms over my chest. "Yes, you know. A man who is quite... *particular* about things. It's nothing to be ashamed of, really. You know what you want, and you demand to have it. I'm sure it doesn't bother a powerful man such as yourself to have that sort of label."

He rolled his stupidly kissable lips. "*What* label?"

I shrugged. "You know... high maintenance. Pompous. Pretentious. *Those* sorts of labels."

His eyes sparkled as his lips turned up in the corners. "Ah. *Those* sorts of labels. You're right, Miss Montgomery—I *am* a man with exquisite taste." His eyes roamed my body from head to toe. I refused to acknowledge what that look did to my panties. "Although, I have been known to go slumming on occasion so I think the drip coffee will be just fine today."

I could feel my face flushing in anger. What an egotistical ass! He was clearly implying that he had been 'slumming it' with me. I wouldn't give him any proof that he was getting to me though.

"Very well. Then, I suppose I'll meet you there after I gather the rest of the materials."

He nodded. "I'll see you there." Before he left, he dug into his pocket and placed something on the corner of my desk. "By the way... I found that on the floor in my office the other night. You might want to ask around and see who it belongs to. Unfortunately, I couldn't really tell you where to begin. There are *so* many possibilities, yet none of them memorable enough to know for sure."

As I picked up the earring—*my* missing earring —I met his gaze. Through gritted teeth, I said, "I'll be sure to do that, sir."

The cocksure smile on his face said it all.

*Checkmate.*

I knew I said I was going with the denial method, but after the stunt that Mr. Maxwell had pulled, I couldn't seem to resist fucking with him. Throughout the meeting, he couldn't keep his eyes off of me. He was subtle about it, but considering we were seated right next to each other, I didn't miss a thing.

Every time I tapped my finger against my lower lip, he would clear his throat. When I shifted in my seat, causing my dress to ride up, exposing my lace thigh highs, he rubbed the back of his neck. Whenever I licked my lips, he gave me the stink-eye. The best one of all, was when I *accidentally* dropped my pen under the conference table and used his thigh to brace myself as I picked it up. I could feel his quad muscle bunching as my fingers came danger-ously close to the growing bulge in his slacks.

Once Mr. Landers, our CFO, finished his slides, Mr. Maxwell excused everyone in his signature tact-less manner.

Just as I rose from my chair, he said, "I need a word, Miss Montgomery."

I fought a smile as I turned around and batted my eyelashes. "Of course, Mr. Maxwell. What can I do for you?"

He waited until the last person left the room before shutting the door. "You can knock it the fuck off."

I blinked innocently. "Whatever do you mean?

What was I doing that could possibly make you so upset?"

His jaw clenched. "Drop the Pollyanna act; we both know what you're doing. It's not only completely unprofessional, but childish. You're better than that, Miss Montgomery."

I glared. "*Unprofessional?* Oh, you mean like fucking your employee on your desk? *That* kind of unprofessional?"

"Watch it," he growled.

"Or what?" I challenged. "You'll spread me out on this table and teach me a lesson?"

He briefly glanced behind me, as if he were considering it. "I wouldn't give you the satisfaction."

I narrowed my eyes. "You're right; you won't. Because I will *never* make that mistake again. Plus, you've already proven you *can't* satisfy me. If I knew you'd be such a lousy lay beforehand, it would've never gone that far."

Mr. Maxwell took a menacing step forward. "Lousy lay, my ass. It didn't seem that way when you were begging for more. *Or* coming all over my dick."

I ignored the current flood below my waist and gave him a disinterested look. "Right. More, as in *better*. I was hoping you'd step up your game. Since you obviously couldn't deliver, I faked it so it would be over faster."

He took another step toward me until my ass hit the edge of the table. "You're a fucking liar."

I patted his cheek condescendingly. "It's sad really; someone so pretty couldn't measure up in the sack. At least now I know why you haven't had a girlfriend since I've known you. Once is *more than enough* for any woman."

With that, I walked out of the room, putting a little extra sway in my hips. When I heard him growling behind me, I muttered under my breath, "You forgot the queen was the most powerful piece on the board, asshole."

# CHAPTER SIX

**RONAN**

I swear to Christ she was doing this on purpose. All week, Miss Montgomery had been especially cold to me but excessively friendly to everyone else. And by friendly, I meant she was shamelessly flirting with every male in the vicinity. Even now, I could hear her chatting with my brother, Liam, fucking *giggling*. Miss Montgomery was *not* a giggler.

She knew Liam was happily married, so I had to believe she was doing this for no other reason than to get under my skin. What's worse is that it was working. Well, fuck her and her manipulation tactics. I was going to put an end to this shit-show.

I opened the door to my office and barked, "Miss Montgomery, socialize on your own dime. The *other* Mr. Maxwell and I have a business meeting that should've started five minutes ago."

Liam's lips twitched as he turned his head in my direction. "Well, hello to you, too, little bro. Quinn and I were just catching up."

I narrowed my eyes at him. "I'm not going to tell you how to run your business, *big bro*, but I'm not interested in wasting time listening to you two gossip." I opened my door wider and gestured for him to come in.

Miss Montgomery rolled her eyes. "It was good seeing you, Liam. Tell Avery I'd *love* to come to dinner."

Now I directed my glare at her. "Why would they invite *you* to dinner?"

She mirrored my expression. "Because your sister-in-law has someone that she'd like me to meet. *For a date*."

"She must not like this person very much, setting him up with someone so frigid."

I didn't miss the way my brother's eyes were volleying back and forth, clearly amused.

Miss Montgomery scoffed. "I assure you I can be *plenty warm* when I want to be."

Goddammit, now my dick was getting hard, thinking about how hot and tight her pussy was. "Doubtful."

Her face reddened. "You unbelievably ego——"

"You're right, Ro. Time is money," my brother interrupted. "Quinn, we'll call you with the details."

He shoved me forward. "Let's get to our meeting, shall we?"

My jaw clenched as I walked into my office. I took a seat behind my desk, preparing myself for the inquisition.

He shut the door. "What the hell was that about?"

"What was *what* about?"

Liam gestured toward the door. "The verbal foreplay with your assistant."

I scoffed and linked my hands behind my head. "Please. Your imagination is running a little wild, don't you think?"

My brother smirked. "Did you forget who you're talking to? I know you better than anyone, Ronan. And I am *positive* you're deflecting. My question is, what are you trying to hide?"

"I have no idea what you're talking about. I don't dip my dick in the company ink."

He barked out a laugh. "Famous last words, bud. I never did either before I met Avery."

I rolled my eyes. "Yeah, well, I'm not you. I would never fall for one of my employees. Just because it worked out for you doesn't mean it was a good idea."

Liam finally took a seat in the chair in front of me. "I never said anything about falling in love. But you *are* fucking her, aren't you?"

I lifted an eyebrow. "Who?"

Now my brother rolled his eyes. "Quinn."

I pushed back images of her pretty pink pussy. "No, I am *not* fucking Miss Montgomery. Nor will I ever be."

He propped his feet on the surface of my twenty-thousand-dollar desk. "So, you'd have no problem if Avery set her up with a client of hers?"

I shoved his feet off and looked him straight in the eye. "Not at all."

"With an A-list actor?" Liam challenged. "One who's been voted People's sexiest man alive? You're telling me you wouldn't mind *one bit* if they went out on a date?"

*What the fuck?* My brother and his wife owned a public relations firm that represented much of Hollywood's elite. It wasn't uncommon for them to arrange dates to drive publicity, but I couldn't think of any reason why my sister-in-law would need Miss Montgomery for that.

I shook my head. "I have no idea why Avery would want to torture the poor man, but I couldn't care less about Miss Montgomery's love life."

Liam sat there for a moment, digesting my words. "Interesting."

Since he obviously wasn't planning to change the subject, I had to do it for him. "Can we cut the bullshit and get on with business? Do you have my press release?"

Liam's New York firm typically managed their

corporate clients, but since we were family, and he was a significant shareholder, my company was the exception to that.

He dug into his briefcase before placing a file in front of me. "It's going out tomorrow."

I looked through the statement announcing our acquisition of two Hawaiian properties—one on Oahu and another on Maui. One of our competitors was struggling, on the heels of a scandal stemming from their former CEO's nasty habit of paying for sex. You could bet your ass I was going to take advantage of their misfortune, especially in a place where tourism was high and vacant commercial land was scarce. "You could've just emailed this to me, you know."

"I know," Liam shrugged. "But then I wouldn't be able to see your ugly mug. I also would've missed that aggressive display of sexual tension between you and Quinn. Avery's gonna love hearing about that."

I clenched my jaw. "Isn't it your job to mitigate false rumors? *Nothing* is going on between me and Quinn." I frowned as I realized my mistake. I insisted on formalities when addressing people around here and my brother knew that. "Miss Montgomery. Nothing is going on between *Miss Montgomery* and me."

My asshole brother shook his head in disbelief. "Whatever you say, Ro. Whatever you say."

∼

Later that day, Miss Montgomery walked into my office without invitation and dropped a thick folder on my desk.

"A knock would've been nice."

She parked a hand on her hip. "If you wanted privacy, you should've locked the door."

I fingered the corner of the file, willing my dick to calm down. "What is this?"

"The new promotional materials you asked for. A thank you would be nice."

I opened the folder and briefly glanced at the brochures. "Don't hold your breath. I'm not going to thank you for doing your job. I think your paychecks do that for me."

Miss Montgomery huffed and crossed her arms, pushing up her ample tits. "Why do you have to be such an ass all the time? Have you ever heard the expression you catch more flies with honey? I know being nice is a foreign concept to you, but you should try it sometime. It sure as hell would make working here much more tolerable."

"If you'd like to lie down on my desk and spread your legs, I'll show you how *nice* I can be." I gave her a leisurely once over, not missing how her nipples perked up at the attention. "With my mouth on your pussy."

She scoffed. "In your dreams."

I gave her a wolfish grin as I rose from my chair and rounded my desk. She turned with me as I approached, her breath hitching as I placed an arm on either side of her.

"What are you doing?" she whispered.

I lightly grazed my knuckles over her perky nipples. "Your body seems to like that idea very much." I bit the fleshy part of her earlobe before whispering, "I think you'd *love it* if I licked your pretty little cunt until your juices were dripping all over my face."

She shivered. "You're a pig."

I wrapped my hand around her slim waist and pulled her into me so she could feel how hard I was. "That may be, but you want me anyway. Your pussy is dripping at the prospect of me devouring you with my tongue. Admit it, Miss Montgomery, and I'll make that ache between your thighs all better."

"Shut. Up." Miss Montgomery grabbed my tie, attempting to yank me down into a kiss.

I lowered myself to the ground instead, putting me at eye level with my target. I pushed her skirt up and buried my nose in her slit, taking a lungful of air, breathing her in. Fuck, I loved how she smelled. "These are the lips I'm more interested in kissing right now."

She moaned as I moved her flimsy panties aside and teased her clit with the tip of my tongue. "Ah... God!"

I swirled my tongue around her hole. "That's Mr. Maxwell to you."

Her thighs clenched as I swung them over my shoulders. "Did you really just liken yourself to God?"

I gave her one long lick from bottom to top. "No, sweetheart. *You* did."

"Unbelievable," she muttered.

Christ, she was warm and wet and tasted sweeter than I could've ever imagined. I could eat her pussy all goddamn day. I brushed my thumb over her slick hole, before moving it lower. I teased her ass while sucking her clit, and she loved every second of it. The only words that left her mouth were curses or pleas for more. Right as she was about to approach the summit, a knock came at the door.

"Go away," I shouted.

"Uh..." the timid voice said through the door. "Mr. Maxwell, I have your lunch order. I'd normally give it to Miss Montgomery, but I can't find her."

She propped herself up on her elbows and whispered, "Shit."

I smiled as I nibbled her inner thigh. "What do you say, Miss Montgomery? Should we invite him in? The door's unlocked. He could turn that handle at any moment and get an eyeful of your soaked pussy, all swollen and greedy for me."

She whimpered as I went back to work on her clit. "Fuck, fuck, fuck."

"You filthy fucking girl," I taunted. "You like the thought of getting caught, don't you? It makes you hot, thinking about the new intern walking in, watching me eat your pretty cunt."

"Shut up!" she whisper-shouted. "He'll hear you!"

The persistent fucker knocked again. "Uh, Mr. Maxwell? What should I do?"

I slid two fingers inside of her, curling them to hit her G-spot. "It's your call, sweetheart."

"Make him go away, you jackass!"

I sucked on her hot flesh, loving the way she squirmed as I did. "Are you sure?"

"Yes, I'm sure, you idiot! Get rid of him and then make me come, for fuck's sake!"

I chuckled before speaking loud enough so he could hear me through the door. "Give it to someone else. I'm already eating my lunch and it's *quite* delicious."

"Um... okay, whatever you say, sir. Enjoy your lunch."

I winked as Miss Montgomery met my gaze. "Oh, I will."

Her head fell back on a groan. "Asshat."

"Now, where were we before we were so rudely interrupted?" I parted her swollen lips with my index finger. "Ah, that's right. I was about to make you scream my name."

She thrashed about, grinding her pussy into my mouth as I switched from licking to sucking to tongue-fucking. My cock was aching, the need to fuck was severe, but worshipping this she-devil's cunt took priority over anything else. If this was my only opportunity to do this, I was damn sure I would make the most of it.

Miss Montgomery's hands were woven deep into my hair as she came, clenching around my fingers, quivering and whimpering, begging me not to stop. Her big brown eyes were fixed on me the entire time, and in that brief moment, everything else faded away. It was disarming—this hold she seemed to have on me. But in that moment, I didn't care. She was fucking magnificent when she came, and I was willing to do anything to see her do it again.

I was quickly learning that I was insatiable when it came to this woman. I couldn't be around her for more than a few seconds without wanting to fuck her raw and ruthless, which was exactly what I intended to do. As I stood, I roughly grabbed her hips, flipping her onto her stomach. After freeing myself from the confines of my pants, I rolled her thong down to her knees and ground my erection into her ass.

I leaned over and bit the shell of her ear. "Hold

on to the edge of the desk. It's going to be a bumpy ride."

I smiled as her body broke into chills as she heeded my command. I donned a rubber as fast as humanly possible and wasted no time guiding my cock into her dripping pussy.

"Fuck," she panted.

Her juices were dripping down her thighs as I rutted into her like a madman. I dipped my hand between her legs, rubbing her slit as I trailed biting kisses down the graceful column of her neck.

I spread her ass cheeks. "One of these days, I'm going to take this beautiful ass of yours."

She moaned. "That's awfully presumptuous of you."

"Oh, really now? And why's that?"

"Because this is never happening again after I leave this room." She yelped as I slapped her ass.

"You say that now..." I bent my knees to change the angle a bit. "But we both know it's only a matter of time before you're begging for my cock."

"God, your ego knows no bounds."

I reached around her to pinch her clit. "It's not arrogance; it's confidence. Big difference, sweetheart."

She arched her back as I rolled her swollen bud between my fingers. "Just shut the hell up and fuck me, you miserable bastard."

I grinned. "Oh, baby, I love it when you talk dirty to me."

Miss Montgomery growled. "I swear to God, if you don't..." She gasped as I shoved myself into her with more force.

I wrapped my fist around her long locks and pulled. "If I don't *what?*"

"Oh, fuck! Keep doing that!" I sped up and yanked on her hair harder. "Fuck, fuck, fuck!"

She clearly liked the hair pulling because she instantly started spasming around my cock. As soon as she stopped clenching, I ground into her a few more times before my balls began to tighten. I pulled out of her and quickly ripped the condom off before shooting my load all over her curvy backside. I trailed my index finger through the cum decorating her skin, down her ass crack, right before delivering one final smack to the right cheek. Damn, I loved the sight of her pinkened skin.

As I headed for my ensuite, I said, "Thanks for lunch, Miss Montgomery. You can show yourself out."

I smiled as I heard a string of curses as I shut the door.

# CHAPTER SEVEN

QUINN

I hated him. I well and truly hated Ronan Maxwell. If I thought he was a miserable bastard before we had sex, I was sorely mistaken. Over the last two weeks, he had been worse than he'd ever been. It didn't help that I was particularly salty lately—for reasons I refused to acknowledge—which meant my tolerance was nil.

The man was on a tirade. Nobody could do right around here. He found a reason to nitpick *everything*. I was pretty sure that everyone in the building was going out of their way to avoid him, which only meant that I was an even bigger target, because I didn't have that luxury.

"Miss Montgomery," Mr. Stick-Up-His-Ass barked, "if you're done daydreaming, I need you in my office *now*."

I gritted my teeth and counted to ten inside my head before gathering my iPad and stepping through his office door.

Mr. Maxwell nodded his head toward the door. "Close it."

I looked behind me before turning back to him again. "Why?"

He narrowed his eyes. "Funny, last time I checked, it wasn't your job to question me."

I glared right back. "Well, sir, considering the outside door to the anteroom is closed, *and* we're the only people still here, I don't really see the point. Not to mention the fact that bad decisions seem to happen in this room when the door is closed."

He abruptly rose from his chair and stomped past me to shut the door himself. Whatever. He could be an ass all he wanted. At least I had the satisfaction of knowing I didn't bend to his little power play.

I casually took a seat and opened the note-taking app on my iPad. Maxwell Hotels focused on sustainability and being as eco-friendly as possible. It was one of the things that set us apart from the other luxury chains. In this office, that meant that we avoided hard copies whenever possible and we only flew commercial for business travel.

"What's on your mind?" I asked.

He lowered himself onto the chair behind his

ridiculously ostentatious desk. "I need you to work tomorrow."

I blinked rapidly, not sure that I heard him correctly. Mr. Maxwell worked at least seventy hours each week, and being his EA, I did the same, but he'd never asked me to come in on a weekend. Not once in the last two years, unless we were on a business trip. Weekends were sacred around here. Working for the corporate office was demanding, and in the interest of employee satisfaction, Mr. Maxwell had always ensured that our entire staff had those two days off so they'd come in on Monday morning fully recharged. It was one of the first things he'd implemented when he took control of the company.

Personality-wise, he was a total dickhead, but Ronan Maxwell took care of his employees. No matter how much you hated the man, you couldn't deny that. Our salaries were more than competitive with perks and benefits that were unmatched within the industry. I'm sure it helped that only a dozen or so people had contact with him on a regular basis, but regardless, our employee retention was one of the highest in any Fortune 500 Company.

Mr. Maxwell drummed his fingers on his desk. "Are you planning to respond anytime this century, Miss Montgomery?"

"Yes, I was going to respond. I'm just trying to

figure out what possible reason you could have for needing me on a Saturday. I had plans."

"Well, cancel them." His dismissive tone was really pissing me off.

I gave him a hard stare. "It's not as simple as that."

He raised an eyebrow in challenge. "Why not?"

I had a date tomorrow afternoon. My first in over a year. I'd been talking with this guy that I met on L.A. Singles and I finally felt comfortable enough to meet in person. We were only planning to meet for coffee, but I was hopeful that could lead to another date for dinner. The excitement that one would normally have for a first date wasn't there, but I chalked it up to a long week. This guy, Micah, was certainly attractive and seemed nice enough so I'd be a fool not to at least try. That was what I kept telling myself anyway.

I cleared my throat. "If you must know, I have a date."

"Is that so?"

I straightened in my chair, not liking his tone one bit. "Yes, that's so. Do you have a problem with that?"

How fucked up was it that I *wanted* him to have a problem with that? God, I needed help. Or a lobotomy.

Mr. Maxwell stared at me for a solid minute,

clenching his jaw. "Fine. You can have the weekend off. Now, get the hell out of my office."

I blinked a few times, shocked that he gave up so easily. I had become so accustomed to the push and pull between us; I was gearing up for a fight. Now, I didn't quite know what to do with myself.

"Did I stutter?" His nostrils flared. "Get. The. Hell. Out. Of. My. Office."

*Well, the attitude is completely unnecessary, you asshat.* But damn, why was I suddenly so turned on, I was tempted to hike up my skirt and ride him? Ever since we had sex, arguing with this man had become a twisted form of foreplay.

I stood abruptly and clutched my iPad over my chest to cover my treasonous nipples. "Are we done for the day, then? It's after nine and—"

"*Go home*, Miss Montgomery. I'll see you on Monday."

He didn't need to tell me twice. I hurried out of his office and down to the parking garage as fast as I possibly could. If I had stayed there any longer, I had a feeling I would've done something really, *really* stupid.

"Quinn?"

I looked up to find my date, Micah, standing next to the table I had sequestered. Coffee already in hand, I must've been spacing out and missed his arrival.

"Hi, it's nice to meet you." I stood up to greet him by placing a chaste kiss against his cheek.

Micah waited until I sat down again, proving that chivalry wasn't dead after all. "I see that you already have a drink. May I get you a refill? Or a pastry?"

I smiled. "I'm good for now, thanks."

Damn, he really was a gentleman, wasn't he? And even better looking in person. Probably about six feet tall, bronzed skin, sparkly green eyes, and shaggy blond hair sprinkled with natural highlights. He wore a t-shirt that stretched across his broad chest with board shorts and flip-flops. This guy was one-hundred percent Southern California born and bred. He could easily be the poster boy for JS surfboards.

Being a Southern Cali girl myself, *this* was the type of guy I was normally attracted to. Hell, now that I thought about it, every man I'd ever dated had similar features. Physically speaking, Micah and I matched. I was your typical girl next door and he was an all-American boy. We'd look *right* together. So, why was I wondering how this guy would look dressed in a designer suit? With darker hair and fuller lips? Ugh, I obviously had issues, that's why.

Determined to not think about my boss, I took a

sip of my iced chai and faced my date. "Did you have any trouble finding this place?"

"Nah," he said. "My condo's actually about a mile away. I love it here. Best cold brew in town."

"Well, I'm glad you didn't have to go out of your way then."

Micah winked. "For you, I'd go the distance." His tone implied he wasn't talking about actual mileage.

I chuckled. "I appreciate that."

He took a sip of his drink. "So, Quinn, what do you do for a living again?"

"I'm an executive assistant in the hotel industry. You mentioned that you were an investment banker, right?"

"I am." He nodded and gestured to his clothing. "Although, at the moment, I seem to be going for beach bum. I hope you don't mind. I can't stand wearing monkey suits a minute longer than I have to."

"I know the feeling." I laughed, motioning to my own attire. "If I'm not working, a tank top and cut-offs are pretty much staples for me."

Micah's eyes dropped to my legs. "For what it's worth, I definitely approve of this loo—"

Movement out of the corner of my eye caught my attention, distracting me from what Micah was saying. "Oh, you've got to be fucking kidding me."

My date scrunched his eyebrows in confusion.

"Is something wrong?" Micah followed my gaze to the two men entering the coffee shop. "Do you know them?"

"Unfortunately." I rubbed my temples to stave off the impending headache. Of course, he would find a way to ruin this for me. Driving me nuts was his superpower.

Before I could say anything further, the man on the left noticed me and smiled. He nudged the guy next to him who, in turn, frowned. Yeah, right back atcha, buddy.

"Quinn!" Liam Maxwell approached our table with a huge grin on his face. "What a nice surprise. What brings you to Malibu?"

I gave him a tight smile. "I'm on a date." Figuring I might as well get this out of the way, I turned toward Micah and gestured to the two men in front of us. "Micah Watkins, this is Liam Maxwell, and his brother, Ronan."

Micah was oblivious to the tension emanating from my boss as he stood to shake his hand. I was pretty sure he figured out something was wrong though when Mr. Maxwell squeezed his hand hard enough to make him wince.

"Whoa, that's quite a grip you've got there," Micah joked. "How do you guys know Quinn?"

"*Miss Montgomery* works for me," Jerkface supplied.

Understanding dawned in Micah's eyes. I'd told

him more than once while chatting online how demanding my boss was. "Ah. Well, it's nice to meet you two."

Liam looked like he was trying really hard not to laugh. "Likewise. We were just grabbing some coffee to go." He gave his brother a little shove toward the barista counter. "In fact, why don't you go order our drinks, Ro."

Mr. Maxwell glared at Liam. "As long as it gets me out of here sooner."

"Do you live around here?" I asked Liam, trying to ignore the murderous glare his brother was sending my way from the other end of the store.

Liam nodded. "I do. Our place is right off PCH about two miles down."

"Nice. So... what are you guys up to today?"

His lips twitched. "We just had lunch at the café next door and now we're on our way to play ball. Just stopping to get an energy boost first."

I raised my eyebrows. "What kind of ball are you playing in dress clothes?" Both men wore slacks and a collared shirt—designer, no doubt—with the top button undone. They looked impeccable, as always, but slightly more casual. Although, maybe casual wasn't the right word. I didn't think these men even knew what that meant. I'd always wondered if they owned normal people clothes like t-shirts or jeans.

He laughed. "Basketball. I have a half court at my house. We can change into shorts there."

"Ah." I couldn't picture my boss wearing athletic clothing, let alone actually playing a game of basketball. Although, now that I was thinking about it, that's *all* I could think about— both men playing one-on-one, shirtless and sweaty, basketball shorts hanging low on their hips.

*Damn*, that was going to be useful later.

Micah cleared his throat. Oh shit, I almost forgot he was here. "That's cool, man. You two have a good game."

Liam smiled at Micah's not-so-subtle brush off. "Right. I'll see you later, Quinn. Avery should be calling you next week with details for dinner."

I nodded. "I look forward to hearing from her. Bye, Liam."

After the Maxwell brothers left the building, Micah asked, "Avery?"

"His wife. She invited me over to their place for dinner. My boss is a dick, but his brother and sister-in-law are pretty great."

"Yeah, your boss seemed really... angry. Is he always like that?"

I shrugged. "Pretty much."

Unless he was screwing me on his desk. He could be pretty damn *friendly* then. Damn it, I shouldn't think about that.

"So... you wanna take these lattes to go?" Micah asked. "Maybe hang out on the beach?"

I looked him over as I contemplated his question. As much as I'd wanted—no, needed—the distraction, it wasn't fair to lead him on. I knew within the first minute of meeting Micah that there wouldn't be a second date. He was a perfectly nice guy, but there just wasn't any spark.

I sighed. "Actually, Micah, would you mind if we cut this short?"

His disappointment was tangible. "Of course not. Maybe another time?"

Gah, I hated this part. "Um... I really don't think that's a good idea. I'm sorry, but I'm just not feeling a connection."

Micah frowned. "Because you're screwing your boss?"

I shook my head. "I'm sorry, *what?*" Did he really just ask me that? "What would possess you to say something like that?"

He laughed mockingly. "Oh, I don't know... maybe the fact that the second he walked in here, your eyes were trained on him the entire time. And his were on you."

"They were not."

*Shit, were they?*

"Plus, I'm pretty sure the dude tried to break my hand when he shook it. Look, Quinn, it's really none of my business, but there's obviously something going on there and as hot as you are, I don't need the drama."

I grabbed my purse and stood, refusing to put up with this any longer. "You're right, Micah. It really is none of your business. It was nice meeting you."

So much for chivalry.

## CHAPTER EIGHT

**RONAN**

"So, you wanna try telling me again that nothing is going on between you and Quinn?"

I dribbled the basketball before making my shot. "Give it up, Liam. There's nothing to talk about."

My brother lined himself up for his own three-pointer. "Bullshit. Then why are you so pissed she's on a date?"

I shoulder checked him as I made my way to the basket. "I'm not. She can date whoever the hell she wants."

Liam grabbed the rebound and held the ball to his side. "Again, I call bullshit. You looked like you wanted to murder the guy. For a moment there, I was afraid I was going to have to bail you out of jail."

I rolled my eyes at his theatrics and gestured for him to pass me the ball. "You can afford it."

My brother's PR firm had exponential growth from the start. Even without his shares in our family's company, he was still worth ten figures.

"Doesn't mean I'd want to," he laughed.

I gave him a dry look and passed the basketball with a little more force than necessary. "Just drop it, all right? I'm done discussing this."

He grinned. "Whatever you say, man."

Liam and I played ball for a good hour before I was ready to call it quits. Physical exertion normally cleared my head, but for some reason, no matter how hard I pushed myself on the court, I couldn't get Miss Montgomery off my mind. I kept picturing her long legs in those obscenely short shorts. Her perky tits beneath that tight top she was wearing. I couldn't stop wondering if she was still on her date —if she and that douche had left the coffee shop. If, at this exact moment, she was fucking him while wishing it were me.

I knew for sure that prick would try getting her into bed. What straight man wouldn't? I swear, everything about her personified sex, with the seductive sway of her hips as she walked across a room. The sugary sweet smell of her skin that made my mouth water. Those cupid's bow lips that she frequently painted red surely just to torture me. She had to know the effect she had on me. As much as I tried concealing the truth, I wasn't *that* good of an actor.

I'd never admit this to my brother, but I *was* pissed that she was on a date. When she'd told me about it last night, I damn near lost my shit. I had to kick her out of my office before I started acting like a jealous boyfriend. The sick thing was Miss Montgomery had every right to date. Logically, I knew that, but that didn't stop me from feeling possessive. If I thought I could get away with it, I would've tied her to my bed so he'd think she'd stood him up.

That thought in itself was ridiculous. Miss Montgomery hadn't given me any indication that she'd be down for another round. In fact, she acted as if it had never happened, for which I should probably be thankful. So, why was I in the office, currently flipping through personnel files on a Saturday afternoon, with the intent of getting her home address?

The woman drove me insane. That was the only plausible explanation.

I'd been sitting in my car down the street from Miss Montgomery's house for over thirty minutes. I was thankful for the foresight to shower in Liam's guest suite before heading out, but on the inside, I was a mess. Hell, I had no idea if she was even home, more importantly, *alone*, but I was sitting here none-theless.

I was on a mission to do whatever it took to get this woman out of my head. I kept thinking that maybe the whole phenomenal sex thing had been a fluke. Maybe if we fucked one more time, it wouldn't be nearly as good as I remembered, and I'd finally get her out of my system. I had to try something. I certainly couldn't continue like this—hating her but wanting her so badly. It was driving me fucking mad.

I marched up the walkway to her little bungalow and banged on the front door. I braced myself as I heard shuffling inside right before the locks disengaged.

Miss Montgomery opened the door a crack. "What are *you* doing here?"

"Are you alone?"

She furrowed her perfectly sculpted brows. "Why does it matter?"

I had to work to unclench my jaw. "*Are you alone?*"

She sighed. "Yes, I'm alone. Now, would you care to tell me why you're standing on my front porch?"

I wasn't going to have this conversation in front of her neighbors, so I pushed the door open and forced my way inside.

"What the hell?" Miss Montgomery shouted.

Oh shit, of course she was wearing nothing but a bath towel. Was the universe fucking with me? A man could only handle so much. "I can't do this anymore."

She clutched the towel like her life depended on it. Unfortunately for me, it only drew my attention even more to the swell of her breasts, rising and falling beneath the cotton. "Can't do *what* anymore?"

I gestured between us. "This. You and me. The constant arguing. The tension. Every-fucking-thing. I can't do it anymore."

Miss Montgomery's big brown eyes narrowed into slits. "I've said this before, but try not being such a jerk all the time. You'd be amazed how nice people would be to you in return."

I rolled my eyes. "I don't give *a fuck* about other people right now."

She returned my eye roll. "Then what *do* you give a fuck about?"

"*This.*"

Before she could say another word, I lunged and slammed my mouth against hers. She opened for me without any hesitation. Her arms circled my neck as our tongues slid sensually against each other's. Needing to feel more of her, I pinned her against the nearest wall and ripped the towel away.

"Oh, God," she panted as my fingers met her

clit. Fuck, her pussy was already soaked, and I'd barely touched her.

I bit her lower lip. "You like that?"

She moaned. "So much."

I gripped her breast with my other hand, rubbing the stiff peak of her nipple between my thumb and forefinger. "And that?"

"Aaah... yeah." She gasped as I thrust two fingers inside her, rubbing vigorous circles over her clit. "I need... ugh... God, I need *more*."

I removed my fingers and smiled against her lips as she whimpered in protest. "When I'm ready. I'm running the show here, sweetheart." Before Miss Montgomery could question me—or kick me in the balls for that matter—I fell to my knees and hooked her right leg over my shoulder.

Her muscles tensed as I ran my finger up her inner thigh. Goosebumps scattered across her flesh as I swept my fingers down the other leg, never quite going where she wanted me to. "Please..."

I nuzzled her thigh, inhaling her musky scent. "Please, *what*, Miss Montgomery?"

She groaned. "Please touch me. Lick me. Suck me. God, just do *something*!"

I met her heavily lidded eyes and winked. "I'm only doing this because I love eating your pussy. Not because you asked."

"I don't care why you're doing it. Just do it!"

Her hands clutched my hair as I began swirling my tongue over her clit. "Oh, right there! Don't stop!"

"So demanding," I murmured.

I licked and nibbled and sucked, until she was squirming so much, I had to hitch her other leg over my shoulder to hold her still. I wanted to memorize every plea, every expletive that leaped off her lips. I wanted to fucking devour every part of her. Ruin her for any other man. I wanted her to look back on this moment, knowing that no one else could ever make her feel this good.

"So damn close," she whispered.

I could feel her impending release, in the way her muscles tensed, how firmly she gripped my hair. How aggressively she rolled her hips, pushing her sweet cunt into my mouth. I thrust two fingers inside of her again, fucking her hard while my tongue worked her nub. Her breaths grew ragged, her moans louder. When I twisted my wrist just right, while sealing my lips over her clit, Miss Montgomery cried out as her orgasm hit. Her legs shook around my head as she rode out the high, screaming in ecstasy.

When she finally came down, I carefully set her legs back on the ground, ready to catch her if they gave out.

She groaned. "You're so goddamn good at that."

I laughed and wiped my forearm against my mouth. "I'm just getting started, honey."

My lips crawled up her body, leaving kisses all over her silky skin. As I reached her perfect handful tits, I closed my mouth over her dark pink nipples, licking and sucking each one until she was once again begging for my cock.

"You're wearing too many clothes," she complained.

I arched an eyebrow. "Do something about it then."

Miss Montgomery started pawing at my belt buckle, hastily undoing my pants as I released each button on my shirt. I reached behind me and grabbed my wallet, retrieving a condom before handing it to her. "Put it on."

She glared at me. "*You* put it on."

Christ, I loved her sass, but she was kidding herself if she thought she'd win this game. I leaned forward and bit the tip of her earlobe. "If you want my dick, Miss Montgomery, you'll put it on." I didn't miss the resulting shiver from my words.

I pushed my pants down just enough to free my cock. Her chocolate eyes glazed over as she watched me stroking myself. "You're an asshole."

"You've mentioned this before." I began moving faster, proving to her that I wasn't going to give in. "I'm perfectly fine coming all over your tits, Miss Montgomery. Either way, the end result is the same.

If you want my dick—which, let's cut the shit, because we both know you do—then you'll rip open that condom and slide it down my shaft." I gave her gloriously naked body a slow once over and my dick jerked in response. "Better decide fast, though. Between your naked body and your attitude, I'm not going to last much longer."

She tore open the foil package. "You're such a bastard. I don't know why I'm even doing this."

I stilled her hand as she slid the condom over me. "Yes, you do. You may not like me, but you fucking *want* me. More than any other man you've met, I'd wager."

She gave me an icy stare. "Just shut the hell up and put your dick inside me."

Miss Montgomery squealed when I lifted her up and wrapped her legs around my waist. "I really don't like being bossed around. You're lucky I'm feeling generous."

"Ha!" she scoffed. "Do you even know what that word means?"

She gasped when I pushed inside of her in one long thrust. "You certainly weren't complaining when I was feasting on your pretty little pussy, now were you?"

Her head fell back as I bent my knees and began moving in earnest. "Just...shut...up...and...fuck...me."

"Funny, I thought that's what I was doing." I

pushed into her with a little extra force. "Do you need me to fuck you harder so there's no question?"

She released an adorable little growl. "I swear you keep talking just to annoy me."

"Payback's a bitch, isn't it?" I smiled and bit her lip. "You two have that in common."

Miss Montgomery slammed her hand over my mouth and glared. Her aggravation only made my dick harder, if that was even possible.

I nibbled her palm until she pulled away. "Hold on."

It was the only warning she got before I ground into her with deep, merciless jabs. It was a little bit cruel, a lot hard, and easily the most erotic experience of my life. Miss Montgomery took everything I had to give with fervor, screaming in pleasure, clawing at my back. I knew the skin right below my neck was torn open, but I didn't care. I wanted her to mark me. I wanted evidence that this was real.

I was getting close, so I reached down and toyed with her clit, until she was a slippery, whimpering mess. I released a muffled groan as she clenched around me, choking my dick until I couldn't hold back any longer. I hitched Miss Montgomery's legs higher on my hips and plowed into her with as much power as I could manage while standing. Within seconds, I was falling with her, into that pleasurable void where nothing else mattered. Nothing but this feeling or this woman wrapped around me. Our situation was as fucked up as it could possibly be, but in that moment, I didn't care.

I slid out of her, carefully grabbing the base of the condom so it didn't slip off. I spotted a powder room adjacent to the foyer, so after tying it off and pulling my pants up, I headed over there to toss it in the garbage. By the time I returned, Miss Montgomery was already shielding herself with the towel, indecision weighing heavily on her face.

I cleared my throat as the reality of our situation sank in. "I think we can both agree that regardless of our mutual attraction, this can't happen again."

It was the last thing on earth I wanted to say, but it needed to be this way. She was like a drug and quitting cold turkey was the only way to go. Whatever this was, wasn't healthy for either one of us.

A flicker of vulnerability flashed across her face before her eyes filled with fire. "Of course not. It was a stupid mistake. One that will *never* happen again. Now, please, get the hell out of my house."

I nodded as I showed myself to the door. "I'm glad we're on the same page. I'll see you on Monday, Miss Montgomery."

# CHAPTER NINE

QUINN

I needed help.

Not only had I once again made the stupidest mistake of my life, but I wanted to do it again. And again. And as many times as I possibly could, before my body couldn't take anymore. I'd spent last night tossing and turning, replaying my most recent encounter with Mr. Maxwell over and over.

When I'd finally fallen asleep, things had gone from bad to worse. I woke up with a start, trembling, aching, on the verge of an orgasm. My dream about my boss had been so vivid, I could practically feel him touching me, still. My clit was throbbing so hard, I could feel my pulse between my legs. All it took was a few quick swipes with my finger and I was falling over the edge, screaming his name.

When I grabbed my phone off the nightstand,

with every intention of inviting Mr. Maxwell over for a roll in the hay, I knew I had a problem. The timing of his delivery couldn't have been worse, but he was right when he'd said we couldn't do this anymore. Clearly my body wasn't on board, so I decided an intervention was in order. People could stage their own interventions, couldn't they? I could no longer keep this to myself, so I had to try something.

Almost every Sunday, I met my two closest friends at this little café in Manhattan Beach for champagne brunch. When I arrived, Sylvie and Antonio were already there, sitting on the oversized patio with a fresh mimosa waiting for me. After greeting them, I sat down and chugged half the drink, needing some liquid courage for what I was about to confess.

"Whoa, slow down there, Lindsay Lohan," Antonio said. "Nobody wants to see you get white girl wasted before noon."

I rolled my eyes. "Very funny."

Sylvie frowned. "Why do you look like shit?"

I rubbed my temples. "Jesus, you two. Is this harp on Quinn day? Can I at least have a minute before you attack?"

Sylvie reached across the table and grabbed my hand. "Honey, what's wrong? You obviously have something on your mind."

I was saved for a moment when the waitress

arrived to take our orders. Since we came here so often, I didn't need time to look at the menu.

"I need to tell you something, but you both have to *promise* not to say a word."

"I promise," they both said in unison.

I took another fortifying sip. "I mean it. Swear on every Gucci accessory you own."

Antonio placed an open palm against his chest. "Ooh, this must be serious."

I nodded. "Dead serious. I did something really... stupid, and I need your advice. But if this gets out, it could be very, *very*, bad, so I need your word that it doesn't leave this table."

"We swear, Quinn," Sylvie promised. "Now, what's going on?"

I sighed. "I had sex with Mr. Maxwell. Three times."

Sylvie gasped. "Say what now?"

At the same time, Antonio started choking on his drink and muttered, "Holy fuck."

I groaned and hung my head in my hands. "I know."

"How in the hell did that happen?" Antonio shouted. "Start from the beginning. And I want *every single detail*, including measurements."

I couldn't help but laugh. Antonio has had a massive crush on Mr. Maxwell since he started working for the company five years ago. Obviously, he knew it was futile, considering Ronan Maxwell didn't swing that way, but I couldn't exactly blame him for his obsession.

I took a deep breath and told them everything from that first encounter in Mr. Maxwell's office. Well, everything minus the intimate details, much to Antonio's dismay. When I finished, my two best friends were uncharacteristically quiet. I fidgeted in my chair, uncomfortable with their silent scrutiny. These two were *never* speechless.

I threw my hands up. "Neither one of you has *anything* to say?"

Antonio held up his index finger. "I need a few moments to process."

I looked to Sylvie. "What about you?"

She cleared her throat. "So, let me get this straight. You're screwing Ronan Maxwell."

"Screwed," I corrected. "Screwing would imply that I intended to continue this... whatever the hell it is."

"O-kay... so you *fucked* Ronan Maxwell. Three times. And not in the same night where you could chalk it up to being a one-off. Three *different* sexual encounters. And even though you hate the man, it was the best sex you've ever had?"

I rubbed my hands over my face. "Yes, Sylvie, thanks for the reminder. I don't need to rehash the details of my epic fuck up. What I need to know is how the hell I'm supposed to move past this? How do I make myself forget this ever happened?"

Antonio fanned himself dramatically. "Honey, if I got Ronan Maxwell into bed, the last thing I'd want to do was forget it ever happened." He sighed wistfully. "He's the only man I'd ever consider bottoming for."

"Ugh, you're missing the point!" I gave him a quizzical look when his last sentence hit me. "Wait... you're normally on top? *Really?*"

He and Sylvie both laughed. "Why is that so hard to believe? Don't get me wrong, I love a little ass play, and I *really* love sucking dick, but by no means am I submissive in bed."

I thought about that for a moment. "Huh. Never would've guessed."

Sylvie waved a hand dismissively. "Enough about Antonio's sex life. I have a really important question."

"What's that?"

Her hazel eyes sparkled with mirth. "Was I right? He's hung like a horse, isn't he? You've gotta at least give me that, Quinn."

I couldn't help the grin that stretched across my face. "He really is."

She threw her hands up in a touchdown pose. "I knew it!"

"But that's beside the point," I said. "Big dick or not, I can never go there again."

"Didn't you already cover that?" Antonio asked. "I don't get the problem. He said it could never happen again, you agreed, that's the end of it."

I shrugged. "It's not that simple."

"Why not?" he asked.

"Because... I've told myself that before and look what happened. Like Sylvie said, one time, I could possibly brush off, but sleeping with him again, and then again, has made this messed up situation so much worse. My attraction to him is like nothing I've ever felt, Tone. There's this constant buzz coursing beneath my skin whenever he's near. It's always been like that, but now that I know how mind-blowing sex with him can be, it's impossible to ignore. It's like every part of my body is attuned to his. I can sense when he's nearby, for fuck's sake. And I *know* that I affect him the same way. I don't think I can go into work tomorrow and pretend like that... *awareness* doesn't exist anymore."

Sylvie gave me a sympathetic look. "Honey, I don't think you really have a choice. Unless you think quitting is an option."

I shook my head emphatically. "No, definitely not an option."

She sat up straighter. "Well, then, you're just going to have to march in there tomorrow with your head held high and be the badass bitch we all know you can be. Just keep telling yourself that you refuse to allow Ronan Maxwell to fuck with your head."

"You make it sound so easy."

She takes a sip of her drink. "It's not. But when you really set your mind to something, you've never failed. If anyone can do it, it's you. You'll just have to fake it until you make it."

Why did I have a feeling that was going to be much easier said than done?

Monday morning had proven to be a complete clusterfuck so far. I came in a little early to gather my wits before Mr. Maxwell arrived. When he walked through my door, he didn't even glance at me, as if acknowledging my existence was beneath him. He simply walked into his office, slamming the door behind him.

Two minutes later, he sent me an email, telling me to cancel all of his morning meetings. When I asked a follow-up question, my email went unanswered. When I buzzed him through the intercom, the only response he gave was a clipped, "You're a bright girl, Miss Montgomery. Figure it out."

I spent the next hour and a half rescheduling everything for later in the week, which wasn't an easy task, considering I had to accommodate other people's calendars. When Mr. Maxwell finally surfaced from his office around noon, I tried getting his attention because he needed to sign some reports, but he breezed right past me again, saying he was headed out to lunch.

Oh, hell no.

I grabbed my purse and practically ran down the hall to keep up with him, smiling in victory when I slid into the elevator right before the doors closed.

I went off the moment we were alone. "What is your problem?"

Mr. Maxwell's stupidly square jaw ticked. "I have no idea what you're talking about."

"Really?" I challenged. "So you haven't been avoiding me all morning?"

He scoffed. "Not everything is about you, Miss Montgomery. I've been busy."

I resisted the urge to punch him in the throat. "Oh, c'mon, do you think I'm stu—"

The elevator stopped one floor down, cutting off our conversation. Of course, since it was the beginning of the lunch hour, by the time we made it halfway down the building, we were all packed in like sardines. You'd think the two people who called the elevator would've waited for the next car, but instead, they decided to force their way in. As bodies shifted around to make room, I was pushed back until my back was pressed against Mr. Maxwell's front.

I had to stifle a moan as I felt his growing erection nestled against my butt.

"Hey Quinn, how've you been?"

I looked in the direction of the voice to find Aaron from accounting. Jesus, could this situation be any more awkward? Aaron was the last man that I slept with before Mr. Maxwell, so I was literally stuck in a steel box between two lovers. This, right here, was why you should never sleep with someone from work.

I smiled. "I'm great, Aaron. How about you?"

He gave me a quick once over. "I'm good. You look incredible. It's been a while since I've seen you, but then again, you were always beautiful."

Mr. Maxwell stiffened behind me and wrapped a possessive hand around my left hip. We were wedged in the back corner so Aaron couldn't possibly see it, but I knew what he was doing—he was marking his supposed territory. Well, I'd show him. I dug the heel of my stiletto into his expensive ass loafers and smiled to myself when I heard a muffled grunt behind me.

"Yeah, I don't get to leave the executive floor too often these days. It was nice seeing you though. Have a good lunch."

Aaron's smile faltered. "Yeah, you too."

Aaron had obviously gotten the hint and turned back around. He was a nice guy, but I definitely wasn't interested, and I wasn't going to use him to get back at my boss.

Said boss's hand was now slowly creeping up the back of my dress. I dug my heel into his shoe even more but lost my footing when he made his way under my lace panties.

I reached out and grabbed the rail when he slipped his middle finger inside of me with no hesitation whatsoever. I should've been pissed that he'd touched me as if he had every right to, but I couldn't, because it felt so good. I could just imagine his shit-eating grin when he'd discovered how shamefully wet I was, knowing it was for him.

The elevator was at capacity, but it still stopped on almost every floor on the way down to the lobby. Each time, we had to wait for the doors to open and then close before continuing our descent. Mr. Maxwell pumped his finger in and out of me the entire time, keeping a slow enough pace to avoid making any noise. I gasped when his index finger began circling my clit, causing the lady in front of me to briefly look back. I could feel my face flushing. I couldn't believe this was happening right now; I was equal parts mortified and aroused.

When the elevator finally—*finally*—reached the

lobby, I couldn't get out of there fast enough. Mr. Maxwell was hot on my tail this time, trying to get my attention without causing a scene. Right before I reached the exit, a familiar-looking woman walked through the door, flashing me a toothy smile. At least I'd thought it was directed at me until she spoke.

"Ronan! This must be my lucky day. Now I don't have to go upstairs to find you."

"Cressida," Mr. Maxwell greeted the busty brunette. "This is a surprise. What are you doing in L.A.?"

I froze.

She pressed her giant boobs into his bicep. "I have a lingerie shoot this afternoon. I thought I'd stop by and see if you wanted to come watch. And if you were free afterward."

That's why she looked familiar! Of course, she was a freaking model.

Cressida leaned into him farther and whispered something in his ear. I couldn't hear what she said, but Mr. Maxwell smirked so I was guessing it was dirty. He briefly looked my way before leaning into her ear to reply. What an asshole! This man literally had his finger inside of me two minutes ago and now he was cozying up to another woman.

I wasn't going to stick around any longer and torture myself. With one final glare, I whipped around and left the building. Well, if I needed an incentive to quit this man, that was it. Fuck him. He could have as many models as he wanted. All I cared about was that he wasn't going to ever have *me* again.

## CHAPTER TEN

**RONAN**

I remember when life seemed so simple. I'd wake up, hit the gym, log a good twelve to fourteen hours in the office, and go to sleep. Occasionally, I'd meet someone like Cressida Cole and have hot, no-strings-attached sex whenever the opportunity arose. I didn't need to worry about anything other than my company, my family, and myself. Life was good.

Predictable, but good.

Ever since Quinn Montgomery had walked into my life, my days had been anything *but* simple. She was always keeping me on my toes. I never knew what she would say or do that would both turn me on and piss me off. That woman had a body made for sin and a mouth made for taping shut. Every day with her was an exercise in patience and self-control.

Obviously, I had deficiencies in both areas.

It had only been one hour since I'd touched her, but it felt like a fucking month. I was acting like a damn junkie, craving his next fix. Willing to do anything to get it. Christ, I finger fucked her in a crowded elevator, in my place of business none-theless, simply because I couldn't *not* touch her. You'd think I would've been able to control myself after spending the morning jerking off in my office, but if anything, that had only made my desire stronger.

All it had taken was one whiff of the vanilla fragrance wafting off her skin and I was half hard. I couldn't stop replaying images in my head of sinking into her tight little body. But it didn't stop at the memories. My fantasies were worse than ever. Now that I knew what fucking her actually felt like, my imagination went into overdrive.

Whenever she spoke, no matter how mundane the topic was, my brain had her moaning beneath me. When she sat in the chair in front of my desk to take notes, I'd picture her hiking up her skirt and pleasuring herself for me. Fuck, the worst was when she glared at me, which was more often now than it had ever been. Seeing that fire in her eyes made me think about releasing all of that pent-up aggression with our bodies. I had fucked plenty of women in my thirty-five years—more than I'd like to admit in my twenties—but no one, and I truly mean *no one*, compared to Quinn Montgomery.

It irritated the fuck out of me.

I scrubbed a hand over my face and sighed. I didn't know where the hell to go from here. The only thing I knew for sure, was that my attraction to my EA wasn't going to go away on its own. I should've taken Cressida up on her offer. She was a beautiful woman and a fantastic lay. Sadly, my dick wasn't even the slightest bit interested. As Cressida whispered her filthy proposition in my ear, all I could think about was finishing what Miss Montgomery and I had started in that elevator.

When her mocha eyes had flashed with jealousy as I'd talked to another woman, my inner caveman puffed his chest out. I wanted to drag her into a dark corner and fuck the envy right out of her. Show her that I didn't want anyone else; that she could have me whenever she wanted. It took a Herculean effort not to chase after her when she'd left the building.

I didn't think it was possible, but each new encounter with Miss Montgomery was even hotter than the one before. I didn't understand how two people who couldn't stand each other could be so explosive in bed. Not that we'd ever got around to using a bed, mind you. Fuck, now I couldn't stop thinking about all the deliciously dirty things I would do to her if I had her spread out on a mattress.

My dick was instantly alert and ready to go. I groaned as I adjusted myself through my slacks, willing the damn thing to go down. Miss Montgomery should be back from lunch any minute and tenting my pants would send the wrong message. Plus, I was determined to avoid any more mid-day jerkoff sessions. I was a grown man, for fuck's sake. I needed to stop acting like a teenage boy who'd just discovered his dad's porn stash.

It was ridiculous the number of times I'd sworn off sex with Miss Montgomery only to throw caution to the wind the next time I saw her. The elevator incident should've been enough motivation to stop, considering how risky that had been for both of us, yet I didn't think either one of us knew how to quench this thirst we had for one another.

Perhaps the only solution was to propose some sort of arrangement. At this point, I thought the damage had been done—it certainly couldn't get much worse. What harm could come from continuing to fuck each other until one or both of us decided they'd had enough? I supposed there was only one way to find out.

Miss Montgomery was acting strange. Ever since she'd returned from lunch, she'd been flitting around the office in an exceptionally cheery mood. We'd had back to back meetings, so I hadn't had the chance to speak to her yet and it was making me anxious. Her unusually sunny disposition wasn't helping matters. It drove me crazy that I had no idea what—or who—was responsible for it.

When we returned from our last meeting of the day, I decided to confront her.

I leaned against the doorway in between our offices. "Why are you in such a good mood?"

She flashed a blinding smile. "Do I need a reason?"

I narrowed my eyes. "Considering you're normally a raving bitch, I'd say yes."

Miss Montgomery returned my glare. "Well, if you must know, I spoke with your sister-in-law over my lunch break and we made plans for the end of this week."

"What kind of plans?"

She started powering down her computer. "Not that it's any of your business, but if you recall, Avery wanted to introduce me to a friend of hers. She's having a dinner party Friday night so we can make that happen. Which reminds me, I'll need to leave by five that day."

"Is that so?"

She locked her desk drawers. "Yes, that's so. I

rarely ask for time off, so my request is not unreasonable, as I'm sure Human Resources would agree. Don't worry; I'll make sure everything is wrapped up before then."

I clenched my jaw. "Didn't you learn your lesson from your little coffee shop friend?"

"*What* lesson?"

I rolled my eyes. "That going out with other men is pointless."

She parked a hand on her curvy hip. "And why's that?"

"Because you and I both know whoever you go out with will never measure up. Like it or not, you'll be wishing he were me."

Miss Montgomery laughed derisively. "You give yourself *way* too much credit. I'd *love* to meet someone who knows how to be a gentleman. Someone who wouldn't be selfish in bed."

My eyes ran the length of her body and back up again. I didn't miss the way her nipples beaded from the attention. "Miss Montgomery, why are you lying to yourself? You don't *want* a gentleman. You want someone who can go toe-to-toe with you. And we both know you're well ahead of me on the orgasm count, so the *last* thing I am in bed is selfish."

She scoffed. "You're delusional, that's what you are."

I gave her a lascivious grin. "If you think

anyone else can own your pussy like I do, maybe *you're* the delusional one."

"Don't you have somewhere to be right now?"

"My dick would certainly like to *be* in your mouth, if you're offering."

"*That* will never happen. But now that you mention it, I'm a *big fan* of blowjobs. If all goes well at this dinner party, I'm sure my date will be more than happy to oblige."

*Over my dead fucking body.*

"It's your loss. Although, now that I think about it, Cressida is *also* a big fan of blowjobs. And she's fan-fucking-tastic at it. The woman has no gag reflex. Plus, she has the sweetest cunt I've ever tasted. We'll probably just skip dinner tonight and go straight to dessert."

I had zero plans with Cressida—or anyone for that matter—but I couldn't resist lashing out at Miss Montgomery. The thought of any other man getting near her with his dick made me insane.

If I wasn't mistaken, she seemed wounded, but that was quickly replaced by rage. "Fuck. You."

I shook my head. "Nah, I think I'll pass now that I have a better offer on the table."

Her face reddened. "Great. Have a *fan-fucking-tastic* time with your model friend. I'm glad, actually, since I'm assuming this means you'll leave me the hell alone from now on."

*Not likely, sweetheart.*

I nodded toward the door leading to the hallway. "I believe you were leaving, were you not?"

Miss Montgomery grabbed her purse and slung it over her shoulder. "Absolutely. I've met my quota for putting up with assholes today. Goodnight, Mr. Maxwell."

The look she gave me before walking out the door said she'd hoped I'd have anything *but* a good night. Unfortunately for me, I had a feeling she was going to get her wish.

The moment I knew she was out of earshot, I walked into my office and dialed my brother.

He answered on the first ring. "Ro, what's up?"

"I need in on this dinner party Friday night."

I scowled when Liam's boisterous laughter carried through the line. "I don't think so."

"Why the hell not?"

"Why the hell would you *want* to come?" he challenged.

I raked a hand through my hair. "I need a reason to spend time with my family?"

"You do when I suspect the real reason you want to attend is because a certain leggy blonde will be there."

I scoffed. "That's ridiculous. This has nothing to do with her."

"Sure sounds that way to me."

"Well, then you need to get your hearing checked."

Liam laughed again. Fucker. "Aw, little bro, are you jealous?"

"No," I denied.

"Right. Well, if it makes you feel any better, don't take it personally. Avery set this up as a couple thing. Everyone who's coming is in a relationship, except for Quinn and Smith."

"Who the fuck is Smith?" I growled. "And what the hell kind of name is that anyway?"

"He's a friend of ours—another publicist. Avery thought he and Quinn would get along, so she decided to play matchmaker."

I frowned. "What happened to 'People's Sexiest Man Alive'?"

I could practically see my brother's condescending grin. "I totally made that up to get under your skin."

"What the fuck is that supposed to mean?"

"Did I stutter?" Liam asked. "I was giving you shit, Ronan. You were getting pissy about Avery setting Quinn up with someone. I saw an opportunity to fuck with you, so I took it."

"You're an asshole."

"So my wife likes to tell me often," he laughed. "Although, you don't really have room to talk. We're cut from the same cloth, you and I. You know, for someone who supposedly doesn't give a shit about Quinn's love life, you seem awfully invested in this whole thing."

"I *don't* give a shit about her love life."

"Uh huh. You keep telling yourself that, bud."

I rubbed the back of my neck, trying to alleviate the sudden tension. "Whatever. I don't have time for this shit."

"Hey man, you're the one who called me."

"God only knows why."

"Because you love me. And I'm one of the few people in your life who tell it like it is. You wouldn't know what to do without me, buddy."

"Yeah, yeah," I grumbled. "I gotta go. Have fun at your *dinner party*."

"Oh, I will. I'm sure Quinn will, too. Bye, little bro."

I threw my phone on the couch cushion beside me as the line went dead. I thought about crashing their dinner party, but only for a second. Liam was fucking relentless when he got a bug under his ass. Always had been. If I showed up at his house Friday night, I'd never live it down. And the last thing I wanted to do was prove him right that I *did*, in fact, give a shit about Miss Montgomery's love life.

# CHAPTER ELEVEN

QUINN

"Quinn, welcome." Avery stepped to the side and gestured for me to enter her home. "Follow me. We're all out back."

We crossed through an open floor plan to a wall of disappearing glass doors. My jaw dropped when I stepped outside and saw their back yard. It had an expansive lawn, colorful flowers, and lush palms everywhere, creating a private oasis of sorts. There was a multi-layered deck, the lower one showcasing a rectangular pool, with an upper deck that held multiple seating options. Off in the distance, I could see a basketball court and I had to push back images of my boss getting sweaty on that patch of asphalt.

"You have a beautiful home," I told Avery. "It

looks like something out of a Home & Garden magazine."

She brushed her long, dark hair aside and smiled. "Thank you. I can't take credit, though. Liam and I work so damn much, we hired designers."

I returned her smile. "Well, you hired well."

Avery laughed as we walked to the outdoor dining area. There was a polished teak table, with miniature Edison bulbs strung along an overhead pergola. I was sure when the sun fully set, they would afford just enough light to see while still remaining dim enough for ambiance.

Avery gestured toward me. "Everyone, this is Quinn Montgomery. Quinn, these are some of our other friends. You already know Liam, and then we have Susannah with her husband, Ted, Ceri and her fiancé, Ryan, Brenda with her husband, Scott, then at the end, we have Smith Walker."

I nodded to everyone in greeting as Avery pointed them out from left to right. The only open seat was right next to Smith, the man I was here to meet. When I approached his end of the table, he stood up to pull out my chair.

"Thank you," I said as I sat down.

Smith smiled. "You're welcome. It's *very* nice to meet you, Quinn."

"You too." I returned his smile.

Smith was definitely interested; of that I had no

doubt. He was an excellent conversationalist too, asking thoughtful, but not too intrusive questions. Every now and then, I'd catch him gazing at me with lust-filled eyes that I so desperately wished I could return. He was certainly a handsome man. Some would even say gorgeous. But was I attracted to him? Nope. Not even a little.

All I could think about throughout dinner was that Smith's eyes weren't the right color—that stunning blue that bled into turquoise as you approached the Caribbean shore. He didn't have a perennial dusting of stubble lining his jaw, like he couldn't possibly bother to shave that morning. His lips were far too thin; I felt zero compulsion to nibble on them.

God, what was wrong with me?

I hated Ronan Maxwell. I could not stress that enough, but when I closed my eyes at night, or when my fingers trailed down my abdomen, ready to give my body the release it so desperately sought, he was all I could think about.

We had an upcoming business trip to tour the new properties. How in the hell was I going to survive that? Sure, we had traveled together quite a few times, but that was before we'd had sex. Although I had fantasized about him for years, I never knew exactly what I was missing before now, which made a huge difference. How was I supposed to resist him when we'd be in such a romantic location? I swore there was just something in the Hawaiian air, where the moment you stepped off the plane, you felt more relaxed. Less inhibited. The last thing I needed was to lower my guard around Ronan Maxwell.

As much as I hated to admit this, he'd hurt me. Logically, I knew that he owed me nothing and I was being unreasonable. We weren't in a committed relationship; he could date whoever he wanted just like I could. And I definitely egged him on—I couldn't seem to stop. But it still stung, knowing he went out with Cressida Cole.

I couldn't figure out exactly when it had happened, but I was emotionally invested when it came to Ronan Maxwell, despite my head's vehement protests. There'd been a persistent ache in my chest since that day. I wasn't a fool; I saw the way she looked at him. There was no way she wouldn't have had sex with him that night. I couldn't stop wondering what they were doing at that very moment. If he was touching her in the same way he had touched me. If she felt like she could never get enough, just like I did. I drank an entire bottle of wine that evening just so I could fall asleep.

Throughout the remainder of the workweek, I went out of my way to avoid him. When we did need to speak, I chose my words wisely. I was careful to tamp down any emotion which had been much easier said than done. Ugh, how was I going to handle working so closely with him in Hawaii, without the buffers that I'd normally have in the office?

Damn it, I was so screwed.

I'd never forget the day I'd met Ronan Maxwell. I had seen pictures of him online, so I knew he was good looking, but I wasn't prepared for the fact that those pictures didn't do him justice. He was so much more imposing in person, and as far as I could tell, there wasn't a single imperfection on that man's body. I'd never been rendered speechless by a pretty face—especially considering Los Angeles was filled with them—but I was absolutely gobsmacked when Edna from H.R. introduced us.

*"And here's your desk," Edna said as we entered the interior office to the CEO's.*

*Just then, the door to the adjoining room opened and Mr. Maxwell walked out.*

*"Oh, good!" Edna exclaimed. "Mr. Maxwell, I'd like you to meet your new assistant. This is Quinn Montgomery. She just finished orientation, so this is her first day on the executive floor. We've already run her through all of the expectations of the position, so she's ready to go."*

*I extended my hand. "It's nice to meet you, Mr. Maxwell. I'm looking forward to working with you."*

*Without saying a word, he eyed my outstretched hand*

*like it contained the Ebola virus. I stood there awkwardly for a good twenty seconds before pulling my arm back.*

*Edna cleared her throat, likely trying to break the tension in the air. "Well, then, I'll leave you to it. Miss Montgomery, all of your access codes are in that file next to your keyboard. A directory with my extension is included as well. Please don't hesitate to call if you have any questions."*

*I nodded. "Thank you so much, Edna."*

*Mr. Maxwell still hadn't spoken a word, so I pasted a big smile on my face and said, "Thank you for the opportunity, sir. I've heard nothing but great things about working for Maxwell Hotels."*

*"Miss Montgomery, for future reference, this is not a casual environment. I expect all employees to address one another in a formal manner." He adjusted his cufflinks as he said this, avoiding eye contact entirely.*

*What was this guy's problem? My friend, Antonio, warned me that our CEO was a tough nut to crack, but I'd never expected flagrant disrespect. He couldn't give me the common courtesy of looking at me when he spoke and the first thing that came out of his mouth was that? I scrolled through the last few minutes in my brain, trying to figure out what I did wrong.*

*Mr. Maxwell raised an eyebrow. "You referred to Ms. Layton by her first name. Going forward, see that you refrain from doing so."*

*"Uh..." I had no idea what to say. I could only stand there like a schmuck with my mouth hanging open.*

It turned out I didn't need to worry about

formulating a response because in the next moment, he'd spun on his heels and marched back into the office, slamming the door behind him. In that moment, I knew that working for Ronan Maxwell might very well be more than I'd bargained for. I knew the man went through a new EA every few months, but I'd always assumed *they* were the problem, not *him*. At least my starting salary certainly made sense after that.

"Miss Montgomery, did you hear what I said?"

I shook myself out of my trance and looked up. Mr. Maxwell was leaning against the doorframe to his office with his hands in his pockets.

"Huh?"

He quirked his head to the side. "How was your weekend? More specifically, the dinner party at my brother's house?"

He looked physically pained by his own question. I bit back a smile and batted my eyelashes.

"Since when are personal conversations permitted in the office? Haven't you told me *hundreds of times* that I was here to work, not gab? Did I miss a memo or something?"

"I'll give you a fucking memo with my dick," he muttered.

I mimed unplugging my ears. "I'm sorry, I didn't catch that. Would you mind repeating yourself?"

"You heard me."

I trained my eyes on my monitor and started scrolling through my calendar. "No, thanks. I have no interest in being anyone's sloppy seconds."

"Jealous, Miss Montgomery?" I'd swear he was smiling, but I refused to look up to confirm that.

I scoffed. "Hardly. Is there anything business-related that you need, sir?"

I did look up this time, raising an eyebrow in challenge.

He pinned me with an icy glare. "Clear my schedule. I'll be out for the rest of the day."

Before I could utter another word, he had already stormed out of the room into the hallway.

Prick.

Fine by me. I wasn't going to complain about not having to deal with him all afternoon.

## CHAPTER TWELVE

**RONAN**

This had to stop.

I couldn't walk away from the office every time Miss Montgomery drove me to the edge of sanity with her backtalk. I wanted to shut her up so badly by tonguing her tight little cunt; I couldn't think of anything else. I had no doubt that if I had, in fact, spread Miss Montgomery out and feasted on her pussy, she would've loved every moment. She would've been livid afterward because she thought I fucked Cressida and was clearly uncomfortable with the thought of me being with another woman, but she would've been begging for more *while* I was touching her.

How was I expected to get any sleep on this upcoming trip, knowing she was in a nearby room with access to a bed? Wondering what she was doing in her free time that we had during the second half of each day. Would she spend hours by the pool or on the beach? Fuck, I could just imagine her in a little bikini, lying on a lounge chair. Her long hair slicked back from a dip in the ocean, skin glistening under the Hawaiian sun.

The mental image had me stroking my cock faster and faster until I blew my load all over the travertine walls in my shower. Christ, I was fucking pathetic. As I turned off the water, I told myself that I had to stop obsessing over her. I'd just have to bury myself in work more than ever so I wouldn't have time to want her.

Should be easy, right?

"I'd like you to add two extra days on Maui."

Miss Montgomery blinked a few times. "Why?"

"I figured since we were already there, we might as well take a couple days off—explore the island a little."

A small crease formed between her brows. "*We?*"

"I don't understand why you're questioning me on this. It's not uncommon for me to build a day off into our agenda so I can check out the local area. I didn't mean *we* would spend that time together,

Miss Montgomery. I would do my own thing and you, yours."

She chewed on that for a moment. "You're right; it's not uncommon for you to take a day or two. What *is* uncommon, is the fact that you've never asked me to change an itinerary before. I'd have to change our flights and reschedule your appointments."

I released a harsh exhale. "I'm staying the extra two days—do what you need to do to make that happen. If you want to keep your original flight, be my guest. But I would highly suggest staying."

Miss Montgomery looked at me thoughtfully. "Why would you want me to stay?"

That was a good question. I didn't even know why I'd suggested extending our trip in the first place. It had been a weak moment on my part—Miss Montgomery had mentioned that she'd never been to Maui before. I couldn't stop thinking about how I'd like to show her some of my favorite spots on the island. Fuck, what was this woman doing to me?

I combed my fingers through my hair. "I *don't* want you to stay, but it would be helpful for business if you'd take advantage of a few of the spa services and give me feedback."

The lie tasted bitter on my tongue, but I sure as shit wasn't going to admit that I did, in fact, want her there with me.

Miss Montgomery nodded. "I'll make the arrangements. May I get back to our agenda before you decide to throw another wrench in the plan?"

Oh, how I'd wanted to teach her sassy mouth a lesson. "Go right ahead."

"So, on Oahu, we land in Honolulu around two in the afternoon. I've cleared that entire day for travel. The next morning, we have a tour scheduled with the on-site manager. That evening, we have the luau. Would you prefer to rent a car or hire a service for transport to and from the airport?"

I drummed my fingers on my desk. "Rent a car. A Jeep Wrangler."

Miss Montgomery looked confused. "But... you normally get a luxury vehicle."

"Don't be such a snob, Miss Montgomery. Jeeps are great vehicles, especially in Hawaii."

My lips twitched when she glared at me. "I'm not being a snob. *You're* the one who always demands 'only the finest.'"

She was mocking me. Deepening her voice and using air quotes on the last three words. Why did I find that so goddamn sexy?

"Be that as it may" —I waved my hand dismissively— "get the Jeep. I want someone that can handle a hard ride."

She shook her head. "Don't you mean some*thing* that can handle a hard ride? You said some*one*."

I bit back a smile. "Get your mind out of the gutter, Miss Montgomery. I assure you, I said some*thing*."

Her eyes narrowed. "Fine. I'll get a Jeep. Now may I move on to our Maui itinerary?"

"By all means. The floor is yours."

As I listened to her rattle off our schedule, I imagined taking her from behind while she was on all fours. Christ, I was beginning to think this would never stop. It was like her pussy had hijacked my brain. Why was this woman so goddamn special?

When we got to Hawaii, I'd have to convince my dick to fuck someone else during our time off, plain and simple. There was always a willing woman looking for a vacation hookup. There was no logical reason why I shouldn't take advantage of that. Fucking someone else had to be the solution. I certainly wouldn't know if I didn't try.

# CHAPTER THIRTEEN

QUINN

"What about this one?" Sylvie held up a deep purple and gold bra. "It's sexy AF."

I took the lacy garment from her. "It *is* pretty damn sexy. It's certainly worth a trip to the fitting room."

She thumbed through the hangers on the rack. "Ooh, and they have matching panties. Thong or boy shorts?"

I studied my options. "Definitely the thong. My work clothes aren't very forgiving with panty lines."

Sylvie moved on to the next display, fingering a racy red number. "What about this? You look fuckhot in red."

I tried not thinking about the fact that Mr. Maxwell loved that color, but I was failing miserably. Whenever I wore any variation of red, it was like waving a flag in front of a bull. He could hardly take his eyes off me.

I shouldn't give a rat's ass what he liked, but I did. If nothing else, it was empowering knowing that I'd be wearing something like that under my work clothes and he'd never have the opportunity to see it. That was the story I was sticking to anyway.

"Grab that one and the red and black one next to it."

"Remind me why we're here again? Didn't you just buy a bunch of stuff a few months ago?"

I shrugged. "I felt like buying pretty things."

Sylvie looked skeptical. "Are you sure this has nothing to do with a certain gorgeous CEO that you're banging?"

"*Was* banging. I'm definitely not going there again after he screwed that model."

She grinned. "If you say so, Quinnie."

I rolled my eyes. "I mean it, Sylvie. I know we never agreed to be exclusive—hell, the only thing we *did* agree on was to not have sex again, and look how that worked out—but it still bothers me."

"Are you sure you're not mostly upset with yourself because that Smith guy didn't make your cooter jump for joy?"

I widened my eyes. "Oh my God, lower your voice! Who the hell says *cooter*, anyway?"

She flipped her hair over her shoulder. "*I do*, and you love me for it."

"It's true; I do," I laughed. "Seriously, though, I don't know what my problem is. It feels like my head is constantly waging war with my body. I honestly don't know how to handle it. No one has ever made me feel like this before."

"Maybe that should tell you something."

"Like what?"

Sylvie held a satin corset against her torso before putting it back on the rack. "Like, maybe you should just give your body what it wants. You're a beautiful, single, twenty-six-year-old woman. He's a smokin' hot, thirty-something single man who knows what he's doing in bed. Your chemistry is off the charts. Why do you have to make it so hard? It's not like we're talking about a dick here."

I chuckled. "Leave it to you to inject a dick joke into this conversation. Also, we sort of *are* talking about a dick. Literally and figuratively."

She shrugged unapologetically. "All jokes aside, I'm serious, Quinn. Why not jump in and enjoy the ride while it lasts?"

"Because he's my boss," I said dryly.

"So? You're both consenting adults. As long as you're discreet, what harm will it do?"

"It could damage my career, Syl. I don't take that lightly."

She contemplated that for a moment. "Honey, I know you don't. But do you honestly think it would? Worst case scenario—let's say you screw each other for a while, and it ends badly. Do you really think Ronan Maxwell is the type of man who would confuse business matters with personal? He seems like someone who clearly knows where one begins and the other ends."

"Yeah... maybe. But I don't know if *I* can separate the two. Plus, I don't even like the guy."

"Your sausage casing sure as hell does." Sylvie winked.

I shook my head, laughing. "Your ridiculousness knows no bounds."

She swung her arm around my shoulder. "It's why you keep me around."

I gave her a side hug. "Thanks for being here, Syl. I don't know what I'd do without you."

She squeezed me back. "Right back atcha, babe."

"I'm sure we could find a *mutually beneficial* solution, Ronan." The woman sitting across the table was practically purring.

I narrowed my eyes as her talon-like nail trailed a path down Mr. Maxwell's forearm. My fists curled under the table when he gave her his signature panty-melting grin in return.

We were at a lunch meeting with Dahlia Vale, the

vice president of Vale Linens, our primary bedding vendor. It was time to renew our contract and they were driving a hard bargain, trying to get an extra fifteen percent. Ms. Vale, the newly appointed V.P., insisted on meeting in person to negotiate.

I had a sneaking suspicion her sole purpose for this meeting was to hit on my boss and he was playing right into her perfectly manicured hands. I was the definite third wheel at this table and quite frankly, that pissed me off. I usually had a much more active role in meetings like this. Mr. Maxwell constantly asked for my input, and sometimes, would let me lead the conversation. Neither of those things were happening now.

I told myself my irritation had *nothing* to do with the fact that Ms. Vale was beautiful, intelligent, and sophisticated—all qualities that a man like Mr. Maxwell would go for. It was purely because I should have stayed back at the office, for all the good I was doing. I couldn't dive into the town car fast enough once lunch was finally over. Although, now that I was stuck in a confined space with Mr. Maxwell, I couldn't wait to get *out* of this car. Unfortunately for me, traffic on the 405 was at a dead stop and we weren't going anywhere for a while.

"What the hell is your problem?" my asshole boss barked.

I shot daggers at him with my eyes. "*You*. You are my problem."

He actually had the nerve to look confused. "What the fuck did I do?"

I caught a glimpse of our driver, Lawrence, watching our interaction in the rearview. Mr. Maxwell must've seen it too, because in the next moment, he rolled up the partition. Lawrence immediately turned up the music, obviously getting the hint.

"Don't worry about it; it's not like you'd really care anyway."

"Spare me the PMS bullshit, Miss Montgomery. I wouldn't have asked if I didn't want to know."

I had to count to ten in my head, so I wouldn't scream. "I'm just wondering why I even bothered coming to this meeting. You and Ms. Vale ignored me the entire time. You literally did not say *one single word* to me. My presence added zero value."

"Aw, were your precious feelings hurt?"

I scoffed. "Hardly. I'm just pissed that you wasted my time."

Mr. Maxwell clenched his jaw. "Let's not forget who works for whom, Miss Montgomery."

"Trust me, I would never forget that," I muttered under my breath. "You'd never let me."

He lifted an eyebrow. "What was that?"

I rolled my eyes. "You're the one who always says I should learn as much as I possibly can in this business. Regardless of your personality faults—of which there are many—the one thing you've always been great at was giving me opportunities to grow. Making me feel like my opinion mattered. That didn't even come close to happening today and it pissed me off. You know damn well I could've held my own in that negotiation, but you were too busy flirting to give me the chance."

He gave me a patronizing grin. "Maybe I decided that assistants were meant to be seen, not heard. That all you had to do was sit there and look pretty and let the real professionals handle the rest."

"*How dare you...* you misogynistic, egotistical asshole! I hate you!" I was too blinded by rage to give my next action any consideration. Before I realized what I was doing, I raised my hand and slapped Mr. Maxwell across the face. The crack reverberated throughout the vehicle. I was pretty sure people ten cars up could hear it.

I think we were both shocked. I sat there speechless as Mr. Maxwell rubbed the spot where I had struck him. The silence stretched before us as his lips thinned and a muscle ticked in his jaw.

"You know..." he began. "You certainly seemed to like me well enough while we were fucking. When you were bent over my desk, loving every second as I pounded into you from behind. Or as you were riding my face, your juices dripping all over my chin. How about when you raked your nails down my back so hard, you drew blood and ruined my three-hundred-dollar shirt? You didn't utter *one single word* of protest then, did you? No, in fact, you couldn't get enough. You couldn't stop screaming my name, begging for more. You seemed to like me *an awful lot.* I'd bet a year's salary that if I reached inside your panties right now, I'd find that you were a slippery hot mess. That your clit was already swollen, begging me to suck on that juicy little bud."

My chest heaved. My pussy ached. I cursed my body for reacting to this man like this. "Fuck. You."

He looked me up and down. "I agree, Miss Montgomery. Fucking does sound like a fantastic plan to temporarily drive the bitch out of you. It hasn't failed me yet."

"In your dreams," I huffed.

"You're right; we do fuck in my dreams. Often." He took his time removing his suit jacket, uncuffing his cufflinks, and rolling his sleeves up before continuing. "You know, playing these games and denying our attraction to one another is getting really old, really fast. I'd much rather spend my time *actually* fucking you than fantasizing about it." He gestured to the obvious hard-on beneath his slacks. "At least I have the balls to admit that. The question is, do you?"

I hated the way my mouth watered at the thought of unzipping his pants and watching his huge cock spring free. How my nipples hardened into sharp points, visible through the thin fabric of my dress. I hated even more how I launched myself into action and started undoing his belt like a woman possessed.

The moment his pants were low enough to free his erection, I straddled his lap. "This doesn't mean I like you."

Mr. Maxwell pulled my thong aside and swiped his finger through my slit. He smiled as he found exactly what he had predicted earlier. "You keep telling yourself that, sweetheart. Your body says otherwise."

I grabbed his length and lined it up with my entrance. "Just shut up and fuck me."

He groaned as I began lowering myself over him. "Condom?"

I shook my head. "We don't need one. We're both clean and I'm on the pill."

He looked at me curiously. "How do you know that I'm clean?"

I moaned as I sunk farther, pausing halfway down to adjust to his width. "Because when your doctor sent over the results to your latest physical the other day, I read the email."

His lips quirked to the side. "You nosy little wench. You're supposed to ignore anything that's flagged as a personal message."

My ass was now in his lap. "Yeah... well... how 'bout we just stop talking?"

Mr. Maxwell fisted the hair at the nape of my neck. "Give me that gorgeous mouth and I will."

He didn't need to tell me twice. Kissing Ronan Maxwell had officially become one of my new favorite things. I groaned as he slid his tongue into my mouth, roughly grabbing my breast at the same time. We started out slow, but that quickly escalated as I lifted myself up until I reached the very tip of him, rolling my hips before sliding back down.

Mr. Maxwell reached behind me and lowered the zipper on my dress, pushing it off my shoulders until it pooled at my waist. He yanked my bra down as well without bothering to unclasp it, leaving it to hang upside down around my abdomen. His pillowy lips formed a tight seal around my nipple, sucking hard enough to leave a sting behind before moving to the other one and doing the same.

As he alternated between kissing and sucking on my breasts and my neck, I wrapped his tie around my wrist for leverage as I picked up speed. In that moment, everything else became insignificant. The only things seeping through my consciousness were the heat of his body rubbing against mine. The ragged sounds of our breathing or slapping of skin. The way he held my hips so possessively, as if he would rather die than let go.

I hated that he could make me feel this way.

That he could have this much power over me. But if I was being honest with myself, there was also a little part of me that loved it. Whenever this man was inside of me, I felt safe, yet at the same time, reckless. He made me feel like it was okay to lose control; that he would be there to catch me if I fell. I had never felt as much freedom as I did when I was with him.

Our bodies were glistening with sweat. The tinted windows were covered in fog. I braced my hands on the inside roof as he grabbed my hips and took control.

"Christ, look at you riding my cock." Mr. Maxwell began moving his thumb in circles over my clit as his eyes remained glued to the spot where our bodies joined. "You're so fucking sexy... you fit me like a goddamn glove. *Nothing* feels better than this."

"Not even Cressida Cole?" I regretted asking the moment the words left my lips, but I couldn't take them back now.

He stopped moving and placed his palms on each side of my face. "Look at me." He waited a moment until I complied. "I haven't fucked Cressida Cole, or any other woman for that matter, in over a year."

He couldn't have shocked me more if he'd said that he shit rainbows and unicorns. "*What?* But... you said—"

He gently pinched my lips together. "I know

what I said. It was a dick move. A knee-jerk reaction to thinking about you with the dinner party guy."

"Why haven't you slept with anyone else?" My voice was so small, I wasn't sure if he could hear me.

He gave me a soft smile. "Because I don't *want* anyone else. I haven't for a long time. As for lunch, I was ignoring you because it was the only goddamn way I could stop thinking about how badly I wanted to be inside of you."

I searched his eyes, trying to determine if he was being serious. When I found nothing but true sincerity shining through his beautiful blues, I was breathless. Ronan Maxwell had just told me that he'd wanted me for over a year. That he hadn't been with another woman because he didn't want anyone *but* me.

*Holy shit.*

I pressed my forehead against his and whispered, "Ronan."

He groaned as his dick jerked inside of me. "Oh, fuck, say that again."

It took me a moment to figure out what the big deal was. I smiled when I realized that I had never called him by his first name before. I circled my hips and glided up and down a couple times before repeating myself. Apparently, the first name basis was really doing it for him because he took control again, thrusting into me harder and faster than before.

We were in such a frenzy that neither one of us could maintain any sort of rhythm, but that didn't lessen the experience. If anything, it *heightened* it. We were so desperate for one another; we were running on pure animal instinct. It was raw and gritty, but it was also intimate. Humbling. If we weren't kissing, we were gazing into each other's eyes. When I climaxed, he brushed his thumb over my jaw and looked at me with so much reverence, so much wonder, I was nearly overwhelmed by emotion.

I didn't know exactly *what* was happening, but it was definitely one of those game changing moments.

Mr. Maxwell tucked his face into the crook of my neck as he chased his release. "Quinn... *fuck*... I don't know how to not want this."

I closed my eyes, loving the way my name rolled off his lips. Resting my cheek against the top of his head, I admitted, "Me neither."

As his orgasm waned, he lifted his head and placed a soft kiss on my lips. "Then, let's not fight it. I'm sick of fucking fighting it."

I was taken aback. "*What?* What do you mean?"

His lips trailed a path down the side of my neck to my bare shoulder. "Let's stop the back and forth. Let's continue doing this—discreetly, of course— and see what happens."

I shook my head. "I don't—"

Before I could finish my sentence, the intercom buzzed.

Mr. Maxwell sighed before pressing the button. "Yes?"

Lawrence cleared his throat. "We've reached our destination, sir."

I blinked rapidly, wondering how that was possible. I didn't even recall the vehicle moving through traffic.

Mr. Maxwell was eyeing me the entire time. "Thank you, Mr. Slater. Give us a few moments. No need to get out; I'll get the door myself."

"Yes, sir."

I quickly climbed off his lap and began putting my clothing back in order. I shivered when I felt the evidence of our encounter drip onto my panties. I couldn't believe we had sex without a condom. I had *never* done that before. And God, we did it in the back of the company car! There was no way our driver didn't know what had just happened. Neither one of us had attempted to keep the volume down. Plus, the unmistakable scent of sex clung to the air. How was I going to face him ever again? What if he told someone?

Mr. Maxwell must've read my mind. As he was tucking himself back into his pants, he said, "I pay Mr. Slater very well for his discretion. You have nothing to worry about."

I bent over to grab my purse. "That shouldn't have happened. I can't imagine what he must be thinking about me right now."

"Who gives a fuck what he thinks about you?"

I jabbed my index finger into my chest. "*I do.* I've worked too hard to be labeled a ladder-climbing whore."

He frowned. "Don't you think you're being a little dramatic?"

Of course, he wouldn't understand. He was the big boss. Nobody would dare question his actions. I, however, was not that fortunate.

"I can't do this." I reached for the handle and opened the door. "I'm not feeling well all of a sudden. I need to leave early."

His blue eyes widened in panic as I began stepping out of the vehicle. "Quinn, don't do this."

Tears pricked at my eyes. "I'm sorry, *Mr. Maxwell.*"

He exited the car and grabbed my elbow. "Just hold on a second. Let's go somewhere and talk about this." I was saved from responding when his phone rang. He swore when he checked the caller ID. "I have to take this."

I gestured to the phone. "Of course. Business first."

He looked hesitant but answered the call anyway. I took that as my chance to escape. Thankfully, our driver had pulled into the underground garage and my car was parked only three spots away. I turned the ignition, wiping away an errant tear. As I drove away from the corporate building, I told myself that I needed to stick to my guns this time. It wasn't worth risking my career for sex, no matter how hot it was. Now, I just had to convince my heart.

# CHAPTER FOURTEEN

**RONAN**

My goddamn assistant had called in sick for the last three days. She had *never* called in before—I'd swear that woman would be drafting spreadsheets from her deathbed if she could. Quinn Montgomery was every bit the workaholic that I was. It was no coincidence that her sudden *illness* occurred immediately after I proposed we continue this... arrangement of ours.

Was the idea truly that repulsive?

That wasn't possible. I had never had chemistry like this with another woman. She enjoyed every second of fucking me just as much as I did with her. I was half tempted to show up on her doorstep and call her on her bullshit. The only reason I hadn't yet was because an irritating voice in the back of my head kept telling me to give her time. That she was a woman, who if pushed, would do the exact opposite of what I wanted simply out of spite. Then where would I be?

We were supposed to leave for Hawaii tomorrow. I couldn't help but wonder if she'd try getting out of it somehow. If that happened, I'd really be fucked, and not in the pleasant sense. She was the best EA that I'd ever had, by a mile. I depended on her to take certain things off my plate so I could focus on the tasks that only I could handle. Her absence over the last few days had certainly not gone unnoticed, but things around here were running fairly smoothly, all things considered. Quinn was organized to an almost obsessive degree —she had backup plans to her backup plans, so we could continue operating as a well-oiled machine, with or without her. At least temporarily.

That didn't mean I was okay with her being gone. I wasn't even the slightest bit okay with *that*.

"Mr. Maxwell?"

"What?" I barked.

"Uh, excuse me, sir, but you weren't responding to my previous attempts to get your attention."

I turned my head toward the man's voice to find our lead receptionist standing in my doorway.

"What do you need, Mr. Vasquez?"

"I have Miss Montgomery holding for you on line three."

"Why isn't my temp telling me this?"

He cleared his throat nervously. "Uh... because she quit about an hour ago."

"*What?*" I roared. "Why the fuck would she do that?"

I'd swear he was holding back a grin. "I believe her exact words were, 'I refuse to work for that pompous ass another second. Tell him I quit.'" When I glared at him, he added, "*Her* words, sir. Not mine."

I scrubbed a hand over my face. Why was it so hard to find good help these days?

I picked up the receiver but didn't press the button since my receptionist was lingering. "Is there anything else, Mr. Vasquez?"

He gulped. "No, sir."

I took the call off hold as I said, "Well, then get out of here. Stop by H.R. on your way back to your desk and tell them I want another temp here within the hour."

Mr. Vasquez nodded. "Yes, sir."

I waited until he closed the door before speaking. "You'd better have a damn good reason for not being here right now."

Her throaty chuckle made my dick perk up. "Still as personable as ever, I hear. How about next time you try, 'Hello, Miss Montgomery. We've missed you around the office. How are you feeling?'"

I rolled my eyes. "Well, *Quinn*, considering I

know damn well you're feeling just fine, that'd be pointless, wouldn't it? You're lucky you're so good at your job or I would've fired your ass for this stunt. Although, I will admit that my cock misses you terribly."

She took a moment before replying. "Why would I call in sick if I were feeling fine, *Mr. Maxwell?*"

I released a harsh exhale. Christ, this woman was infuriating. "Can we please cut the bullshit? Those of us who actually showed up for work today have things to do. In case you've forgotten, we're scheduled to leave in the morning, so I have quite a bit to accomplish beforehand."

"Of course, I haven't forgotten," she snapped. "That's why I was calling, actually. I wanted to let you know that I'm meeting you at the airport instead of taking the company car as planned."

"Why would you do that? Afraid you can't control yourself alone in a car with me? You do realize we're going to have *plenty* of alone time together during this trip, don't you?"

She scoffed. "Get over yourself. This has nothing to do with *that*."

"Oh really?" I challenged. "Then, give me one good reason why you can't use the service that you've already scheduled?"

"Because I don't want to. I'm getting a ride from a friend."

"*What* friend?" I growled.

"That's really none of your business, Mr. Maxwell."

I rubbed at the tension coiling in the back of my neck. "Would you quit with the Mr. Maxwell bullshit? I thought we've moved past this."

"We most certainly have *not*."

"Really? Well, you *most certainly* didn't have any trouble using my first name the other day. '*Oh, Ronan*, just like that. *God, Ronan*, you feel so good. *Fuck, Ronan*, I'm going to come.'" I smiled, even though the sassy wench couldn't see me. "Any of *that* ring a bell?"

Quinn released an adorable little growl. "Are you done? Can we get back to business now?"

I picked up a pen and twirled it between my fingers. "Fine."

"Like I was saying earlier, I *will* meet you at the airport. The driver will be at your condo to pick you up at quarter to nine. I'm going to check us in online right after I get off this call, but I need to know how many bags you're checking first."

"One. Is that it?"

"Yes, that's it. I should be there shortly before you arrive, so I'll meet you by the baggage check area. I'll see you then."

I clenched my jaw. "I have one thing to say before you hang up."

She sighed. "What's that?"

"Don't think for one second that you're off the hook, *Quinn*. I'll be more than happy to remind you how much you love screaming my name when I see you tomorrow."

I didn't give her a chance to reply before ending the call. If she thought we were going back to formalities, she had another thing coming. I was *not* going to tolerate this cat and mouse game anymore.

Fuck me, this was going to be a long flight. When I arrived at LAX, I headed straight for the baggage check area and spotted Quinn. I rarely had the opportunity to see her dressed so casually, but whenever I did, I had to fight an erection the entire time. Today, she was wearing those obscenely short denim shorts again and a sleeveless top that hugged her tits perfectly. I shouldn't have been surprised—she almost always wore shorts and a clingy shirt whenever we flew to warmer destinations.

It damn near gave me a heart attack every time.

I'd made several requests—okay, more like demands—that she'd adopt a more business casual attire on our travel days. So far, she had yet to comply. I wasn't proud to admit this, but I'd never fought back on the matter for the simple fact that she looked fucking hot like this. I'd seen this woman in fitted Gucci dresses, sexy as hell Prada pantsuits, and even completely naked as of recently, but there's something about how well that cotton molded to her curves that really got me going.

Like I said before, this was going to be a *long ass* flight.

I stuck my hands in my pockets to adjust myself as I approached her. "Quinn."

"Mr. Maxwell." She tilted her chin up as she handed me a luggage check tag. "I've already dropped my suitcase, so once you put that on and drop yours, we're good to go."

I secured the tag to the handle on my suitcase and gestured for her to walk with me to the drop off window. I placed my bag on the scale and waited as the attendant reviewed my documents.

The woman handed my driver's license back to me. "Have a great flight, Mr. Maxwell."

I nodded. "Thank you."

Quinn stiffened and took a few steps to the side when I placed my hand on her lower back to guide her.

"I can walk just fine by myself, thank you very much."

I leaned into her ear and didn't miss the resulting shiver. "But then I couldn't touch you and that's not nearly as much fun."

Quinn grabbed my arm and yanked me to the side so we weren't blocking foot traffic. "Would you stop?"

"Stop what, *Quinn?*"

"That!" she huffed. "The touching. The first names. Stop all of it. This is a business trip that I'd like to keep *strictly business. Capiche, Mr. Maxwell?*"

I gave her a glacial stare. "I've already told you that I'm done playing these games with you. What part of that did you not understand?"

She rolled her eyes. "This isn't a game. It's my job! *And yours*. All I'm asking is that you act like it. Treat this like any other business trip we've taken before... before we..."

I leaned closer and lowered my voice. "Before you enthusiastically bounced on my cock? You know, the same one you recently admitted that you couldn't get enough of?"

Quinn ground her teeth together. "Add dirty talking to the list of things you should *not* be doing on this trip."

"But you *like* my dirty talk." I winked. "Don't even think about trying to deny that."

She flushed, confirming my statement. "It doesn't matter. That's in the past and I'd like to leave it there."

I stretched my neck from side to side. "You're a fucking liar."

"And you're an asshole!"

I smirked. "Why, Miss Montgomery, that wasn't a very professional thing to say to your boss."

Quinn rubbed her temples. "Jesus-fucking-Christ, you're driving me crazy."

I gripped her elbow and started walking. "Join the club, sweetheart. Look, why don't we agree to disagree for now? I really don't want to spend the next five hours on a plane with you while you're so pissy. You can have it out with me when we get to the hotel."

Considering fighting always led to fucking with us—at least lately—I found myself looking forward to it.

She shook off my hold as we stepped into the security line. "Fine."

Since we were flying first-class, getting through security was a breeze. With almost ninety minutes to kill, I suggested we grab breakfast in the lounge and surprisingly, Quinn agreed. The first thing she did when we got there was order a bottle of champagne with a carafe of OJ.

"We're drinking mimosas, I take it?"

Quinn stabbed herself in the chest with her index finger. "*I* am drinking mimosas. If you want some, get your own."

I laughed. "I think I'll stick to coffee."

She shrugged. "Suit yourself."

An egg scramble for each of us and nearly three mimosas for Quinn later, her frosty demeanor warmed a bit.

"You know, it wouldn't kill you to loosen up."

"How so?"

"Did you really need to wear a suit when all we're doing today is getting on a plane and checking into the hotel? Do you even *own* any t-shirts or jeans? Or, God forbid" —she pressed her open palm against her chest and gasped,— "shorts?"

I hid a smile behind my coffee mug. She was adorable when she was being a smartass.

"I own quite a few of each." I widened my eyes for a dramatic effect. "I even packed some shorts in my suitcase!"

Her eyes narrowed. "Liar. We've been to several tropical destinations now and you've always worn slacks."

"I guess you'll just have to wait and see." I checked the time on my watch. "We'd better get going. They should be boarding by the time we get to the gate."

Quinn lifted her champagne glass and chugged the rest of the mimosa. I had to fight the urge to lick the tiny droplet that escaped from the corner of her mouth. She dabbed her mouth with a napkin, flushing as our eyes met. It was likely from the alcohol consumption, but for the sake of my ego, I'd hoped part of that was arousal.

We both rose from the table at the same time. Quinn wobbled a bit, automatically reaching for something to stabilize herself. That something just happened to be my bicep.

I reached out with my other arm, pressing into the curve of her spine. "Whoa there, take it easy."

She managed to catch her balance but was still holding onto my arm for dear life. "Sorry. I guess the champagne hit me all at once. Thankfully I ate some food, huh? At least you don't have to carry me to the gate."

I leaned down and whispered, "I wouldn't have minded. Although, I'm pretty sure they won't let you on the plane if you're shit-faced, so I *am* glad you ate." I nodded toward the pastry case. "Maybe you should grab a croissant or two to help suck up the liquor even more."

Quinn's flush deepened. "Not a bad idea."

"You're much more agreeable when you're drunk, you know." My lips pulled up in the corners.

She glared. "Shut up. I am *not* drunk."

I picked up a small paper bag and a pair of tongs. "Whatever you say, sweetheart. You want anything else while we're here? A chocolate muffin, perhaps?"

Quinn had a weakness for chocolate muffins. Every time we brought pastries in for a meeting, she discreetly wrapped one in a napkin and set it aside.

She gave me a soft smile. Fuck, she was beautiful when she did that. "Sure. That would be nice."

After filling a to-go bag with two croissants, a

Danish, and a chocolate muffin, I threaded her arm through mine, which she actually allowed. After a quick pit stop to use the restroom, we arrived at our gate. They had just started boarding the first-class cabin, so we walked straight up to the attendant and scanned our tickets. My fingertips pressed into Quinn's spine as we made our way down the ramp and into the plane. I stowed our carry-ons in the overhead bin as she settled into her window seat.

After folding my suit jacket over the armrest, I dropped into the seat beside her. "You doing okay?"

"Yeah." She retrieved a pair of earbuds from her purse before stowing it beneath the seat in front of her. "A little tired, actually."

"Why don't you rest for a bit?" I suggested. "I'll wake you up when they start serving lunch."

Her eyes briefly fluttered closed. "Yeah... okay. That works."

She was out cold by the time the plane reached cruising altitude. I powered up my laptop and immersed myself in mind-numbingly boring reports. I was trying desperately to ignore the sleeping beauty beside me, but that quickly became a futile attempt.

I was continuously distracted by her soft little murmurs. The way her mile-long legs kept shifting. How her pouty lips were slightly parted into the shape of an O. At one point, chills broke out all over her skin, so I covered her with my jacket. She instantly snuggled into it and I could swear, she even released a little moan. I was being bombarded with one memory after another, none of which were conducive to deflating an erection.

I didn't know how I was going to survive four more hours of this.

With a heavy sigh, I shut down my computer and tucked the tray table back into the armrest. Maybe Quinn had the right idea by taking a nap. I didn't normally sleep well on airplanes, but it was worth a shot. Anything would be an improvement over my current agony.

I was painfully erect and no matter how hard I tried, it wouldn't go away. I couldn't even excuse myself to the restroom to take care of it because I was tenting my slacks. God forbid, I actually had to take a piss. I had never been more grateful for inflight blankets than I was now. It was much easier to avoid indecency charges with the fleece draped over us.

I reclined my seat and extended the leg rest, careful not to wake her. I groaned when she curled up on her side and rested her head against my shoulder. It was an unconscious move on her part but having her this close to me was making the situation worse. Fuck, she smelled good.

I tucked some loose hair behind her ear, and she scooted into me further, curling her hands around my bicep. I found myself smiling at the knowledge that Quinn Montgomery was a cuddler. For some reason, I hated the fact that I didn't know that about her before now.

I knew that I should probably move her off of me, but then I would risk waking her, and it was in my best interest that she remained unconscious. I decided to take my own advice instead and rest for a while, since I couldn't focus long enough to get any work done. Besides, it was easier to avoid the temptation of touching the woman beside me—or staring at her like a creepy stalker—if I were asleep.

This woman was going to be the death of me, I swear.

# CHAPTER FIFTEEN

QUINN

I startled awake, wincing as a crick in my neck made itself known. My eyes blinked rapidly as they struggled to focus. Once the sleep fog had finally cleared, I noticed that Ronan was snoozing quietly beside me. Damn, I loved his name. I loved thinking it and saying it, especially in the heat of the moment as he'd so crudely pointed out earlier. Why did I insist on going back to formalities? Why was calling him by his first name such a big deal? People did it all the time, especially ones who had seen each other naked. Although, now that I thought about it, I'd never actually seen Ronan completely naked before.

I made a note to myself to rectify that ASAP. Wait... scratch that. That train of thought could only lead to trouble. I had no idea how to handle this new dynamic of ours, but one thing I was certain of, was that Ronan Maxwell was trouble with a capital T. That was why I'd insisted on calling him Mr. Maxwell earlier, and why I needed to continue doing so. It helped me maintain the wall around my heart that seemed to be weakening every day. It was pretty much my last defense in protecting myself from this man.

God, he was so arrestingly beautiful like this. The persistent chip on his shoulder was nowhere to be found. He looked significantly younger than his thirty-five years on any given day, but in sleep, it was even more prominent. He had this innocence about him that was boyish, almost, but with a rugged, manly twist. I had to fight back the urge to lean forward and pepper his stubbled jaw with kisses.

"If you're going to keep staring at me, you might as well take a picture," he mumbled.

Shit! How long had he been awake? And how did he know I was staring?

"Please. I wasn't staring." I schooled my expression as his eyes opened.

His lips curved. "Okay, sweetheart, let's go with that."

"Don't call me that." I narrowed my eyes. "It's demeaning and entirely inappropriate in the workplace."

He looked around the cabin. "Funny, I thought we were on an airplane, not in the office."

"You know the point I was trying to make."

His eyebrows rose. "I'm afraid I don't."

Jesus, I wanted to smack him. "Fine, be an ass. Since you need me to spell it out for you, if you need to address me for any reason, Miss Montgomery will suffice."

Ronan released a short laugh. "Good luck with that... *Quinn*."

"Nuh-uh." I shook my head. "We're not on a first-name basis. How many times do I have to tell you that?"

"And how many times do I have to tell you that's not going to happen. I'm not going backward."

My hands curled into fists. I swear, I'd never met someone who could elicit so many violent thoughts before him.

"You are the most stubborn person I've ever met."

He glared. "I could say the same about you, *sweetheart*."

Ugh, I wanted to scream. Since that wasn't possible, I decided avoidance was the best solution. I folded my arms and turned to look out the window.

I almost jumped when I felt his hot breath on my ear. "Listen to me, because this is the last time

I'm going to say this. I will agree to your request when we're conducting business, while other people are present, but that is the *only* concession I will make. If we're alone, anything goes." When I opened my mouth to argue, he placed a hand on my thigh, rendering me speechless.

"I've been inside of you. I know how warm, wet, and tight your pussy feels as it clenches around me. I know how fucking sweet it tastes. I know that your nipples are a dusty shade of pink and that you whimper whenever I wrap my lips around them." His hand slid up a little farther. "I know that you have a small birthmark on your inner thigh, an inch to the left of your delicious cunt. I know that you think of me at night as you're getting yourself off. I know that your fingers —or whatever toys that you may have in your arsenal—will never be enough, because it's *me* you want. It's *me* you crave.

"Whether you like it or not, that's a fact; there-fore, I say we *are* on a first-name basis. You're arguing with me just for the hell of it at this point. I get it; you're a strong woman. You're probably the strongest woman I've ever met. That said, quit fucking fighting me on something so trivial."

Dear Lord, I didn't think my panties could be any wetter.

"I can't seem to help myself. You bring out the worst in me," I whispered.

He nipped the shell of my earlobe. "Likewise. But all the orgasms make up for the aggravation."

I shivered. "It's still not a good idea."

"Why not?"

"Because you're my *boss*."

Ronan gently pinched my chin, prompting me to turn toward him. "Not when we're like that. We're just two people enjoying each other's bodies."

"It's more complicated than that."

His thumb traced my bottom lip, and I had to resist the urge to pull it into my mouth. "Do you trust me?"

I gulped, trying to ignore the tingle his touch left behind. "Not especially."

He gave me a wry look. "I'm being serious. Our personal association will in no way affect our working relationship. You know me well enough to know that I don't deliver false promises. If I say I'm going to do something, I will always do everything in my damn power to make that happen."

I knew he was right, and I did actually trust him, but that didn't make it any easier to give in. The more tangled our web became, the more certain I was that this man had the power to break me. Despite his assurances, I wasn't sure if *I* was capable of compartmentalizing like that.

"Excuse me, we're about to start serving lunch. Would you two like to look at the menu?"

Ronan pulled away. "Yes, please." He handed

me the little card that listed our food choices. "Well?"

I briefly glanced at the menu and decided on the fruit and cheese platter. Once the flight attendant was gone, I turned to Ronan. "I need time to think about it."

He contemplated that. "Fuck that. You'll only talk yourself out of it. If you can't fully commit to it right now, then give me Hawaii. Let's take advantage of our time away from headquarters to relate on a personal level. Let's toss the boss-employee component out the window when we're off the clock. I'll try not being so much of an asshole if you agree to dial the bitch down." He smiled when I glared at him for that last comment. "If either one of us decides that it won't work after we return home, so be it. Just give me the week."

I took a deep breath and decided to throw caution to the wind. "Okay."

"Okay?" He smiled.

I nodded. "*Just* Hawaii. Then we can reassess."

"Deal."

God, I hoped I didn't regret this.

We were stuck in traffic again; this time Ronan was driving though, so there was no chance of repeating what had happened the last time we were on a freeway together. Although, I couldn't say the idea wasn't appealing. We rented a Jeep as he had requested, and he insisted on driving with the top down. I didn't know why, but seeing this man behind the wheel, dark hair blowing in the wind, my lady bits were taking notice. His sleeves were rolled up and I couldn't stop fixating on the way his forearm muscles flexed as he gripped the wheel. Or on the small patch of exposed skin where he'd unfastened the top two buttons on his shirt.

"Did you really pack shorts?"

He quickly glanced at me. "Why are you so obsessed with my wardrobe all of a sudden?"

"Because... you must be uncomfortably warm right now with the top down. Who the hell wears a suit on a tropical island without air conditioning?"

"I do, apparently."

I rolled my eyes. "No shit, Sherlock. My point was, if you truly did pack island appropriate clothing, why aren't you wearing it? You could've changed before we got into the car. I'm barely wearing anything and I'm roasting."

His Ray-Bans slid down the bridge of his nose as his eyes leisurely roamed my legs. "So I've noticed."

My cheeks heated. Thankfully, I could blame the weather if I had to. "So? Are you going to answer my question?"

He laughed. "Because I wasn't about to dig

through my suitcase in the middle of the airport and then change in a goddamn bathroom."

"Why not? People do it all the time."

"I'm not most people."

You could say that again. No other person could piss me off and turn me on in the same breath like he could.

I kicked off my flip-flops, reclined my seat, and propped my feet on the dash. I didn't miss the way Ronan's eyes tracked every motion. That was the good thing about being at a standstill in traffic, I supposed. You didn't need to worry about distracted driving if you weren't actually moving.

"Whatever. Sweat to death for all I care." I closed my eyes and turned my face toward the sun.

"Would you prefer if I were naked? Because that could easily be arranged."

My lips quirked. "I'm sure."

A light breeze crossed through the Jeep as we inched along the H-1. I loved this place—been here a dozen times—but that was the one downside of Oahu. With nearly the entire state's population residing on this one island, plus all the tourists, it took forever to get anywhere in the Honolulu-Waikiki area. If you ventured outside of the city though, it was fine.

"You just say the word and consider it done, sweetheart. My dick is at your command."

I fought a smile. Man, he really wasn't kidding

when he said we'd drop all the boss-employee pretenses. He'd been incredibly flirty ever since, playful even. It was hard not to follow suit. The change was so drastic; if he wasn't still cocky as fuck, I'd think aliens had inhabited his body. I could easily see myself falling for this Ronan. I took a deep breath as I shook off that scary thought.

I must've fallen asleep because the next thing I knew, we were at the hotel. Ronan pulled up to the valet and shifted the Jeep into park.

"Have a nice little nap?" His lips turned up in a teasing smile. Damn, he was pretty when he did that.

I smothered a yawn as I sat up. "The champagne must still be in my system."

The valet opened my door. "Good afternoon. Welcome to the Maxwell Waikiki. Are you checking in?"

I took his hand and stepped out of the car. "We are. Our reservations are under Q. Montgomery."

Whenever we traveled to a Maxwell hotel, I always booked the rooms in my name since it wouldn't stand out nearly as much as our CEO's. Ronan insisted on experiencing everything as a guest would and that would be impossible if he threw his name all over the place. Every once in a while, an employee would recognize his face, but for the most part, he was able to fly under the radar.

The man made a note on the valet tag as Ronan

handed him the keys. "Very well. We'll get your bags loaded and sent up to your room immediately."

Ronan shook the valet's hand, leaving a tip behind. "Thank you."

I hitched my purse over my shoulder and jerked my head toward the entrance. "I'm going to check us in."

"I need to call the office. I'll meet you inside in a few minutes." He pulled his phone out of his pocket before walking down the sidewalk a bit.

I used the self-service check-in kiosk and stood to the side, waiting for Ronan to return. A good ten minutes later, he finally showed.

"Everything okay?" I asked.

His brows pinched together. "Yeah. I'm just thinking about everything I need to do today. I didn't get any work done on the plane."

We started walking toward the elevator bay. "Anything I can help with?"

He shook his head. "No, I've got it. You should relax. What floor?"

I held out his keycard. "Seventeen."

Ronan nodded as he took the card from my hand. The elevator had just arrived by the time we got there, so we stepped into it once the car had cleared out.

"Are you sure I can't help?"

He gave me a look that I couldn't quite decipher. "Why don't you go check out the pool area for me? Kick back and relax, maybe order a few of those fruity drinks you like. Take note of the service and you can give me the recap tomorrow."

"Um... okay, if you're sure."

He nodded. "I'll probably just get some room service and power through the most important stuff."

I told myself not to be disappointed that he didn't want to spend our free night hanging out. I should've expected it even; this man was a workaholic through and through. I thought I was bad, but at least I had no problem indulging in some R&R while in a place that practically demanded it.

I shrugged my shoulders. "Suit yourself."

Our rooms were adjacent to one another's so as we stood in front of each door, I was practically holding my breath, waiting for him to change his mind. Ronan held his key in front of the electronic pad and turned the handle once it unlocked. So much for that idea.

He stepped over the threshold. "I'll see you later."

That was the last thing he said to me before closing himself inside his room. I walked into mine, angry with myself for letting this bother me so much. Whatever. I was in paradise, and I was damn well going to enjoy my limited time off, with or without that stupidly sexy man.

# CHAPTER SIXTEEN

**RONAN**

I shouldn't have been there. My attention really should've been on my business, but I couldn't stop thinking about the fact that Quinn was likely sitting by the pool, wearing a bikini. Wondering if she looked as good as I'd imagined. Before I could talk myself out of it, I had powered down my laptop and changed into a pair of swim trunks. Now, here I was, scanning the pool deck, trying to find the beautiful blonde who'd tattooed herself on my brain.

The area was pretty empty since it was close to sundown, so it didn't take long before I spotted her standing at the edge of a crescent-shaped infinity pool. Quinn was looking out toward the harbor, so she hadn't noticed me yet. As I waded through the shallow water, she tilted her face toward the setting sun. The watercolor sky gave her skin an almost heavenly glow, accentuating her delicate features. She lifted her body from the water just enough to expose her breasts, making me pause for a moment to appreciate the view.

Jesus, she was stunning.

She was clad in a bright red and white floral bikini. It wasn't one of those little triangle suits that barely covered a woman's nipples. Not that I'd ever complain about seeing her in one like that, but this suit couldn't be more perfect for her. It was sexy as hell but also somewhat modest, hinting at the treasure that laid beneath.

When I was about five feet away, she must've sensed the disturbance in the water because she turned to see who was approaching. As her eyes landed on me, they widened in shock and her pouty lips formed into an O. I grinned as I came closer, amused by her reaction. I also didn't mind the fact that she couldn't seem to take her eyes off my bare torso.

I didn't stop moving until I was so close, I had her caged in against the edge of the pool. "Hi."

She blinked a few times. "What are you doing here? I thought you had work to do."

"I do." I ran a finger along her bare shoulder, down her arm. "But I couldn't stop thinking about you."

"Why not?"

Her voice was breathy, a sure sign of her arousal. If that wasn't evidence enough, Quinn's nipples hardened under the thin material of her swimsuit as my hand continued its descent. I stopped just as it landed on the curve of her waist, with the tips of my fingers pressed against the little dimple on her back.

I bent down to place a soft kiss on her cheek. "Because we had an agreement." I grabbed her hand below the water and placed it on the bulge at the front of my shorts. "I've been hard as a rock, thinking about all the filthy things I'm going to do to you this week. There was no way in hell I could get any work done until this was taken care of."

Quinn stroked my cock through my swim trunks. "Is that so? What makes you think I'm interested?"

I pressed closer, grinding my erection into her stomach as I whispered in her ear. "Sweetheart, we both know that you want me inside of you as badly as I want to *be* inside of you. That you *need* my thick cock stretching that tight little cunt of yours."

I wasted no time reaching behind her and diving my hand beneath her bikini bottom. Quinn gasped as my finger slid between her round cheeks, pressing briefly against her puckered hole. "You dirty girl, you like that, don't you?"

Her spine bowed. "Maybe."

I chuckled as I reached farther and teased the

opening of her pussy. "Has anyone ever taken your ass, Quinn?"

She squirmed as I pushed the tip of my finger inside of her cunt. "No."

I could feel my control slipping, so I pulled my hand out and took a step back, leaving her with a dazed look on her face. "That'll make it even better when I do."

Her mouth gaped. "I never agreed to that."

I grinned widely. "You will."

A flush spread across her chest and up her neck. I had to resist the urge to tear off her top and suck on her tits in front of all these people.

"You are the most arrogant man I've ever met."

"So you've said. Can we move on to the fucking now?"

She chuckled and shook her head. "No. Let's see how you behave at dinner before I decide on that."

I smiled. "Dinner, huh?"

"Yep." She nodded. "I think you should at least buy me dinner before you try getting in my pants."

My lips twitched. "It's cute that you think I have to *try*."

"Ha ha, funny guy." She rolled her eyes again before turning away from me toward the sunset.

I pulled her back against my chest. "There's one thing I've never been accused of."

Quinn's laughter died on a moan when I nipped

the shell of her ear. She rested her hands over my bare forearms, scoring my skin with her nails. "I can't believe you're not wearing a designer suit right now."

I held her tighter. "That might be a little odd considering I'm in a pool."

"Nah, I think this is weirder."

"Wiseass." Since we were faced away from any potential onlookers, I took advantage by dusting my fingers over her nipple through her top.

Her head fell back on my shoulder. "God."

I pressed my erection into her body. "There's plenty more where that came from."

"Save it for later, you ass. Now, stop groping me and let me watch the sunset."

"You're no fun," I teased.

It took a great deal of self-control, but I managed to keep the groping to a minimum as we watched the sun make its final descent across the sky. As it dipped below the horizon, Quinn released a heavy sigh.

"Absolutely breathtaking."

I glanced down at the woman in my arms, wondering how I managed to get here. "I agree."

I wasn't talking about the sunset.

She broke away from my hold and made her way to the other end of the pool. "Pick me up in an hour."

"What?" I chased after her. "Are you sure I can't interest you in a little dessert first?"

Quinn grabbed a towel from a nearby lounge chair and began drying herself off. "Nuh-uh. I need to wash the chlorine out of my hair and change into something more appropriate for dinner."

I gave her an obvious once over. "Appropriate is overrated."

She threw her towel at me and pulled a gauzy dress over her head. "Too bad. Pick me up in an hour and not a minute sooner."

With that, she slipped on her shoes and started walking away, leaving me grumbling behind her as I dried myself off.

Exactly one hour later, I was standing in front of Quinn's room, ready to knock on the door. Before I had the chance though, she opened it.

"Well, I'll be damned; you do own regular people clothes."

I smirked. "I always pack clothes like this in warmer locations. You've just never seen me during our time off."

I was dressed in a navy-blue polo with beige cargo shorts—a far cry from my usual attire. To be completely honest, I enjoyed wearing suits. They made me feel powerful, plus I looked considerably younger than I actually was, so dressing well helped with perception in the business world. But Quinn seemed to have this preconceived notion that I was incapable of letting loose and if being more casual tonight would help my cause, so be it.

I wanted her to see that I wasn't always the hardass she knew at the office. That there was more behind the man that I allowed the public to see. I'd wanted to show her this part of me for a long time now, but since she worked for me, I couldn't afford to let my guard down. Now that I thought about it, the frustration I felt over that was probably the main reason I was such a jerk to her. I figured if I pushed her away, if she hated me—or better yet, quit—the temptation would be easier to fight.

I had taken over the company when I was thirty-one; far younger than most CEOs of multi-billion dollar empires. I lived and breathed Maxwell Hotels for as long as I could remember, but I still had to prove that I deserved my position. Every damn day, I'd worked my ass off to prove that I earned the role fair and square. That nepotism did not exist in my company. My father would've never left me in charge of his father's legacy had I not been fully qualified, but there would always be doubt. There would always be someone who assumed the job was handed to me on a silver platter. I would always be swimming upstream trying to prove myself.

It was a cross I bore willingly because I truly loved this company. I actually gave a shit about our guests' experience. Sure, I was competitive by nature and wanted to be the best, but making my father proud, providing for my future children, helping my employees provide for *their* families, that was my top priority. *That* was why I worked so hard.

"Ronan, where'd you go?" Quinn was waving her hand in front of my face.

"Sorry, I was trying to picture what you looked like under that dress," I lied.

She wore a simple black cotton dress with sandals. Her long hair fell freely down her back and the only makeup she had on from what I could tell, was some light pink lip gloss. Everything about her was understated, but in my opinion, she was magnificent.

Her chocolatey eyes twinkled with humor. "Well, you're going to have to keep wondering. I'm hungry."

I grabbed her by the wrist and yanked her into me, catching her off guard. "Me too."

Quinn placed her open palms on my chest as she caught her balance. "What are you doing?"

"This." I clutched the back of her neck and closed the remaining distance between us. There was nothing gentle about the kiss. It was pure possession—a prelude to all the naughty things I planned on doing to her tonight.

"Wow... um..." She touched her lips with the tips of her fingers. "What was that for?"

I took her hand in mine and led her to the elevator. "Just getting it out of the way so I didn't have to think about it all through dinner."

"Oh. Okay, then." She gave me a soft smile.

I didn't want to worry about being interrupted in one of the on-site restaurants, so I decided to take Quinn to a nearby establishment. Waikiki Beach had a high walkability index, so instead of getting our rental from the valet, I threaded her arm through mine and guided her to the main drag that ran parallel to the Pacific.

I nodded to the entrance once we reached our destination. "Here we are."

Surprise registered on her face when she saw that we had stopped at a local bar & grill. "Huh. Not what I was expecting."

I raised my eyebrows. "Would you prefer we go somewhere else?"

"Not at all." She shook her head. "This is perfect."

I placed my hand on the small of her back and guided her into the restaurant. We were seated on the back deck which overlooked the ocean. Since it was dark, our view was limited, but you could see the waves crashing against the shore and smell the salty air.

"God, everything looks amazing." Quinn looked up from her menu. "What are you getting?"

"I'm thinking the Kalua pork tacos."

"Ooh, I was debating between that and the macadamia crusted Mahi Mahi. How about you give me one of your tacos and I'll split my fish in half?"

I nodded. "Sure."

Whenever we worked through dinner—which was fairly often—Quinn almost always sampled some of my food. My lips curved into a smile when I recalled the first time she'd done that. We had ordered takeout and halfway into our meals, she reached across my desk and swapped her drunken noodles for my pad thai without saying a word. I sat there, speechless, as she dug into my entrée with gusto. When she looked up and saw that I wasn't eating, she shrugged and said, "Deal with it." It was the first time she'd ever shown sign of a backbone with me. It was also the first time I'd imagined throwing her on my desk and fucking her into oblivion.

"What are you smiling about over there?" She took a sip of her pink cocktail.

"I was just picturing you naked again."

Quinn shook her head. "You and the nakedness. Is that all you ever think about?"

"Lately, it does take up the majority of my thoughts," I answered honestly.

She laughed. "Well, to be fair, I can't exactly blame you. The naked time is fun."

I grinned. "That it is."

I liked how effortless this was. As much as she fought me on it, Quinn seemed to have no trouble setting business aside. There was no need for propriety. Our constant bickering was nonexistent. The drinks flowed as we ate and the more alcohol she consumed, the flirtier she became. By the time our plates were cleared, I didn't think the sexual tension between us had ever been higher. I couldn't wait to get back to the hotel so we could actually do something about it.

The elevator ride to our floor was painfully long. We had to stop on almost every level to let someone out. When we were finally inside her room, my patience snapped.

I pushed her against the door and started trailing kisses down her neck. "How drunk are you?"

She moaned as I bit down on the spot where her neck met her shoulder. "Not drunk enough to not know what I'm doing."

I pulled back to verify the truth in her statement. I knew consent wasn't an issue; every other time we'd been together, we were both stone-cold sober. And while drunken sex had its merits, that wasn't what I was going for. Tonight, I wanted this woman's full attention. I needed to know that she would remember every little detail of what was about to happen. When every muscle in her body ached tomorrow morning, I wanted her to visualize all the dirty reasons why.

Quinn's eyes were a little glassy, her cheeks slightly rosy, but she definitely had her wits about her. She looked like she was gearing up for a fight should I dare challenge her.

I grinned. "Excellent answer."

Her returned smile made my chest ache. There was so much goddamn joy behind it. She had *never* looked at me like that before. Like *I* was the source of her happiness. It made me want to strut around like a proud peacock—the one with the tallest and brightest feathers in the flock. Quinn stared up at me for several long, loaded beats. Neither one of us said a word, nor were we in any hurry. We just absorbed the moment, perfectly content just being near each other.

*Fuck, this woman makes me feel unhinged.*

I ran my thumb over her cheek. "What is it about you? Why do you make me feel like this?"

She turned her face into my palm. "Like what?"

"Like a fucking superhero. Like I can do anything. Like I *would* do anything, just to see that smile on your face."

Her mouth dropped open and her eyes went wide. "That's the sweetest thing anyone has ever said to me." She gave me a sassy smirk. "Although if I ever repeated that, nobody at work would believe that it came out of your mouth."

"Let's just keep it between us then, huh?" I winked.

Quinn laughed and slowly traced her index finger across my eyebrow and over my jawline, before landing in the middle of my chest. I closed my eyes when her warm hand slid down my abdomen, curling her fingers under the waistband of my shorts. "Ronan?"

I bent low so our foreheads were pressed together. "Yeah?"

"I need you to fuck me now."

She squealed when I lifted her up and tossed her on the mattress. "Yes, ma'am."

# CHAPTER SEVENTEEN

QUINN

"So... tell me about your past exploits."

Ronan released a deep belly laugh. Damn, he had a good laugh. "*Exploits?*"

He wrapped his arm around me as I snuggled closer. "Yeah. I want to know about the women of your past."

"Is this your way of asking how many women I've slept with?"

I propped my chin on his chest, meeting his eye. We'd been lying in bed talking for the last two hours. The sun had risen just enough to allow us to see each other clearly. "Not really. I mean, I probably don't want to know the answer to *that* question. I'm more curious if there was ever anyone serious in your life?"

He tucked a piece of hair behind my ear. "I was married once. Is that serious enough for you?"

My eyes widened in surprise. How did I not know that? "Really? When?"

"Right before I started grad school. We had dated all through college; we were your typical young and hopelessly stupid couple. We thought nothing could touch us."

"What happened? How long were you married?"

His shoulder lifted. "Less than a year. There was never any one big event. I guess you could say that we realized our differences were insurmountable. We grew up together, ran in the same circles, but we never had much in common. When we both ended up at Columbia, it was convenient, I suppose, to have someone you already knew in a land of strangers." He gave me a crooked grin. "Plus, I was eighteen; I had sex on the brain 24/7 and she was hot."

His muscles clenched as I trailed a finger down his abdomen. "So, not much has changed there. Go on."

Ronan pinched my butt, making me yelp. "Anyway... as I was saying, I started my internship with the company's New York office shortly after we got married. She thought I worked too much—didn't understand why I was so invested in such a lowly position. Why I didn't want to live off my trust fund like she did and party around the world. Over time, I became increasingly frustrated because she didn't get it."

"That your last name didn't get you the job?"

He looked at me thoughtfully. "Exactly."

"Eventually, Kylie—that's her name—finally had enough and filed for divorce. The funny thing about it was that I don't think either one of us really cared. If anything, we were *relieved*. Since then, I've had... *arrangements* here and there, but never had time to manage an actual relationship. Found it was easier to avoid them altogether."

I kissed the spot in between his pec muscles. "Is that what you want with me? An *arrangement*?"

"*Hell, no*." Well, this was awkward. I tried pulling away from him, but he tightened his hold on me. "Not so fast there." He tilted my chin up. "You're different, Quinn. What I want with you is... unprecedented. Ineffable."

"Right," I scoffed.

He searched my eyes. "Why are you doubting me? You know I'm not a bullshitter. Look... I'm not exactly a hearts and flowers kind of guy, and I can't make any promises, but this thing between us *is* different and I'm tired of pretending it's not. You're not some fleeting interest; I meant it when I said that I've wanted you for a long time. And now that I've had you... now that I know what I was missing... I definitely don't want to give that up. I sure as fuck don't want any other man putting his hands on you."

I smiled to myself. "So... you want monogamy?"

"Fuck yes, I want monogamy."

I shifted my body until I was straddling his lap. Since we were still naked, I could easily feel his growing erection beneath me. "Okay."

His fingers dug into my hips. "Yeah?"

I rolled my hips, sliding along his length. "Yeah."

Ronan groaned. "What about your *past exploits*?"

"Not much to speak of." I gasped as the flared head of his cock rubbed against my clit. "Had a steady boyfriend in high school, another in college, but in both cases, we knew we'd go our separate ways after graduation. Since then, I've dated, but nothing serious. I wanted to focus on my career." I moaned when Ronan took my nipple into his mouth, sucking and biting it before releasing me with a pop. "In case you haven't noticed, I'm a lot younger than you."

"Not *that* much younger," he argued.

"Plus," I continued, "there was this guy I was attracted to. Painfully so. I didn't really think it was fair to pursue something with anyone else while that lingered."

I was still rubbing myself back and forth, coating Ronan's dick with my arousal.

His pretty blue eyes narrowed as he shifted our

bodies until I was perched over him. Pulling me over his cock in one smooth motion, he growled, "*What* guy?"

God, why did I find his inner Neanderthal so hot? I couldn't resist poking the bear. "He's a major asshole, actually. And so cocky it's almost unbearable at times. But for some reason, I couldn't stop wondering what it'd feel like, taking him into my body, riding him until we both exploded." I demonstrated by rolling my hips, sliding up and then back down. "I wanted to know if his pretty mouth was good for anything other than delivering barbs or barking orders."

By this time, it was obvious Ronan had caught on. Mainly because he no longer looked like he wanted to maim somebody. "Did you ever find out?" He grabbed my hips and started thrusting into me from below. "Did he live up to your fantasies? Did he fucking own this pussy? Ruin it for any other man?"

"Mmm, and then some."

"Oh yeah? Better than me?"

"*So* much better," I teased.

"You're going to fucking pay for that, you little witch."

Before I knew what was happening, I was suddenly on my back, with my legs thrown over his shoulders. Ronan showed no mercy—not that I was complaining—pounding into me hard and fast, with no signs of slowing down. My back bowed off the bed, meeting him thrust for thrust. Our skin glistened with sweat, the sounds of bodies slapping echoed throughout the room. I was positive his fingertips would leave bruises on my hips. This was sex in its most primal form. Raw, gritty, and incredibly dirty.

"This pussy is *mine*." Sweat dripped down his temple as he picked up the pace. "*Mine* to fuck. *Mine* to taste." He grabbed my butt cheeks, spreading them wide. "This virgin ass is *mine* to take. No other man will *ever* have that pleasure, if I have anything to say about it." He palmed my breasts. "These gorgeous tits are *mine*. I'm the only man who gets to lick them, or suck them, or slide my dick between them." He moved to my lips, tracing them with his thumb. "These lips are *mine* to kiss." He pushed his thumb into my mouth, imploring me to suck. "*My* cock is the only one that gets to come inside this mouth. *My* tongue is the only one that gets to tangle with yours." Ronan leaned closer until my knees were pressed against my chest and his lips were a hairsbreadth from mine. "You get what I'm saying here, Quinn?"

I tried to say yes, but I'm pretty sure it was more of a groan. Jesus Christ, no one had ever *claimed me* like such a caveman before. As much as it offended my feminist sensibilities, I couldn't say I minded it one bit.

He smiled. "Good. I'm glad we cleared that up. Are you ready to come now?"

"*So* ready," I panted.

Ronan braced one hand on the bed and used the other one to make circles over that tiny bundle of nerves. "Hold on, baby. I'm not going to be gentle."

"Good. Don't."

My arms flew over my head to grip the headboard. Blood thundered in my veins as he resumed an unyielding pace. Ronan watched my face the entire time, as if he were memorizing every little freckle. The way my lips parted as he rubbed my clit. How my eyes rolled back when he sank one knee lower into the mattress, deepening the angle. How the telltale flush of arousal scattered across my flesh as my orgasm violently ripped through my body. Not once did his ocean-colored eyes stray.

As my climax faded, he pulled out and flipped me onto my stomach. Ronan licked a trail down my spine, nibbled the generous globes of my ass, sucked the skin on the backs of my thighs. He sank back into me so deep, a slew of expletives flew out of both of our mouths. His powerful thighs clamped around mine, pushing them together, making our fit impossibly tight. With his hand on the middle of my back, pressing me flat into the mattress, he fucked me so hard, I wouldn't be surprised if there were a permanent imprint of my body on the bed when we were done.

I screamed his name as I spun out of control once again, and only moments later, Ronan did the same. I didn't think either one of us could move as we caught our breath. My body felt like Jell-O; every single muscle screamed in protest. After a while, he pulled out of me with a shudder and rolled onto his back beside me.

"Fuck," he muttered as he turned his head in my direction.

"Yeah," I agreed, not really capable of stringing together sentences at the moment.

Ronan grabbed my hand and brought it to his mouth to kiss my knuckles. "You're pretty fucking incredible, you know that?"

"You're not so bad yourself."

"You know what else?" He leaned closer, a conspiratorial gleam in his eye.

"What?" I whispered.

He brushed a patch of sweaty hair away from my face and placed a gentle kiss on my forehead. "I think we've nailed this relating on a personal level thing."

I smiled. "I think so, too."

The next morning, I awoke to an empty bed. I reached over and touched the rumpled sheets beside me. They were cold, so I knew that Ronan had been gone for a while. I couldn't say I was surprised, but I was more disappointed than I'd like. Dozens of images floated through my mind as the reality of what had happened yesterday hit me.

*Holy shit.*

I told myself not to panic, but I still struggled to find my breath. Last night, the sex had been incredible as always, but there was this level of uncharted intimacy. With every touch, every kiss, and every word, Ronan had allowed me to see a side of him that I never knew existed. When he spoke about his ex-wife and his need to prove his worth at work, he was so exposed, yet he trusted me enough to offer that information. I was positive he rarely, if ever, shared such private thoughts.

How could so much change after only one night?

I climbed out of bed and made my way into the bathroom. Ugh, my body ached *everywhere*. It felt like I'd been ridden hard and put up wet. I startled when I caught sight of my reflection in the mirror. My hair was a disaster, as it should be after a night of marathon sex, but it was everything else that gave me pause. My lips were swollen. My eyes were *wild*. Tiny little patches of red dotted my skin where Ronan's unshaven face had pressed against it. I smiled when I spotted the R-shaped hickey on my inner thigh.

*Such a caveman.*

My phone pinged with a new text message from said Neanderthal. When I opened it, I saw that it was actually the second message he had sent me. The first one was from an hour ago, explaining that he was heading to his room to shower and dress.

*Bosshole: Just checking in to make sure I didn't fuck you into a coma.*

Only he could make such a crass statement cute.

*Me: No coma here. You'll need to try harder next time. I'm about to jump in the shower.*

*Bosshole: *Groans* Great. Now my dick is hard.*

I chuckled.

*Me: So join me and do something about it.*

*Bosshole: Sweetheart, I wish I could. I'm already down-stairs—needed some real coffee before we got started for the day. Someone kept me up most of the night.*

I checked the time and realized that our meeting with the hotel manager started in forty-five minutes. Shit, I needed to get a move on.

*Me: I'll be down ASAP. Grab me an iced one.*

*Bosshole: Hazelnut or vanilla today?*

I smiled. Ronan had *never* bought me coffee before. We'd shared a lot of meals together, but I always grabbed my own coffee before heading to the executive floor for the day. The only way he could've known what I liked to order was if he paid attention to the cups that sat on my desk.

*Me: Hazelnut please.*

*Bosshole: See you in a bit. If you feel the need to play with yourself in the shower, make sure you set your phone up and record it for me.*

I shook my head.

*Me: Ass.*

*Bosshole: You love it.*

My lips twitched.

*Me: Maybe...*

*Bosshole: Stop texting me and get ready so I can see your sexy ass in person.*

*Me: Yes, sir, Mr. Maxwell, sir.*

*Bosshole: You're getting spanked for that one later, wiseass.*

Was it bad that I was actually looking forward to that? I set my phone on the nightstand and headed for the shower, knowing that if I continued this conversation, I'd never make it to our meeting on time.

## CHAPTER EIGHTEEN

**RONAN**

If my site manager didn't stop hitting on Quinn, I swear to Christ, I would kick his ass. We'd been touring the property for almost an hour and he had been getting increasingly flirtier by the minute. He was still on the right end of professional —most likely because I was present—but I'd about had it.

I held my hand up to cut off whatever the hell he was saying. "Mr. Hamilton, will you excuse us?"

He cleared his throat. "Of course. Is something the matter?"

Quinn gave me a *what the fuck are you doing* look, but I ignored her.

"Yes, everything's fine." I thumbed through the emails on my phone. "I just received an email from headquarters, and I need to address it."

"I can continue with Mr. Hamilton if that helps," Quinn offered.

If I thought she was actually trying to be helpful, I'd be fine, but the look on her face told me that she was fucking with me because she knew I was up to something.

I narrowed my eyes at her. "Miss Montgomery, I'll actually need your assistance with this." I turned to Mr. Hamilton. "We were almost finished touring the grounds anyway, right? I wouldn't want to hold you up; I'd rather let you get back to business. Miss Montgomery and I have already visited the pool area and we can easily stop in the spa when we're done taking care of this urgent matter."

"Of course, sir." Mr. Hamilton nodded and pulled a business card from his pocket. "If you need anything, my personal cell number is on there."

I took the card from him. "I appreciate it. Now, if you'll excuse us, we really do need to address this."

"What is going on?" Quinn whispered harshly as we were walking away.

I led her down the hallway to an empty conference room. Once inside, I locked the door and slammed my mouth into hers.

"Whoa, what's that about?" she asked as I pulled away.

"Going forward, I'm going to need you to stop flirting with the on-site staff."

She narrowed her chestnut eyes. *"Excuse me?"*

I flung my hand toward the door. "That guy was checking you out the entire time! You weren't helping the situation by wearing that dress or being so goddamn friendly."

"Did you really just imply that it's *my* fault he was leering at me because of what I'm wearing?" Her face reddened. *"You ass!"*

I rubbed the back of my neck. "What? *No.*"

My eyes traveled the length of her body. Today, she was in a light pink linen dress that had a large floral pattern on it. It hit her about mid-thigh before flaring out into a ruffle-type thing. It was an aloha style dress so totally appropriate for the circumstances, but the way that it showcased her curves combined with her stiletto sandals, she was turning heads everywhere we went.

"Well... maybe," I admitted. "I didn't fucking like the way he was looking at you."

"Unbelievable," Quinn muttered. "You know, I might be okay with the caveman routine in the bedroom, but it's *not* acceptable under any other circumstances, especially work. What happened to exercising self-control while on the clock?"

I tugged at my hair. "You make me fucking crazy."

She growled. "Yeah, well, I'm not so fond of you right now either. You're being an epic dick."

"What did you say?" My voice was low. Menacing. I advanced upon her until Quinn's back was pressed against the wall.

A storm was brewing in her eyes, but the rest of her body was reacting to my sudden proximity. The pulse in her neck was pounding, her lips were parted, and her nipples were peaked. Christ, I loved how responsive she was.

"You heard me, you bastard."

I leaned down and sucked her lower lip into my mouth. "Mmm, your lip gloss tastes like sugar."

"What are you doing? We're having a conversation here."

I ran my hands down her arms before anchoring them on her tiny waist. "I'd much rather do this."

She gasped as my lips moved down to her rapid pulse. "Ronan, you can't solve everything with sex."

"Mmm, but it'd be fun trying." I wedged my knee between her thighs.

Quinn rubbed herself against me. "Was there even an email from headquarters?"

"Several, actually. But nothing that needs my attention right now." I winked.

She shook her head. "Stop trying to be cute. I'm pissed at you."

I raised an eyebrow. "Would it help if I apologized?"

"I don't know. You've never tried it before."

I smiled as I took her face in my hands. "I *am* sorry. I don't know what came over me. I've never been so... possessive before; I wasn't thinking clearly. That's not an excuse; just an explanation. I will try to control the urge to throat punch my staff in the future."

She bit her lip, fighting a smile. "That's much better."

I jerked my head toward the door. "Can we go upstairs and get naked now?"

She shook her head. "Always with the naked."

I held the door open for her. "We have seven hours before the luau. I plan on making the most of them."

Despite my attempts to keep Quinn in bed and skip the luau, she kicked me out of her room so she could get ready without my *grabby hands*, as she called them. So, here we were, in the middle of the dinner portion of the event, sampling a little of everything.

"Oh my God, this is the best teriyaki chicken I've ever had."

I grinned. "It better be. I didn't hire a three-star Michelin chef to design the menu for nothing."

"And Maui has the same offerings?"

I nodded. "We're claiming to have the best luau on each island. That means the best show *and* the best food."

She took a bite of rice. "Damn, even the fried rice is exceptional. How could something so simple be so good?"

"Because I hired the best. And he doesn't come cheap—nor do the quality ingredients; hence, why we *will* continue charging our guests for admission."

Quinn laughed. "Ah, the argument that started it all. Good times."

I looked around to ensure we still had privacy. I had a table set off to the side of the main dining area so we could discuss the menu items freely.

"You keep looking at me like that and I'm going to crawl under this table and dine on your pussy."

Her eyes widened. "You wouldn't dare."

"Try me," I challenged. "The show is about to start. No one is going to pay attention to the two people lurking in the shadows."

"Speaking of the inciting incident to all of this" —she gestured between us— "what's going to happen when we get back home, Ronan?"

My brows furrowed. "What do you mean?"

"Well, *if* I decide I'd like this thing to continue... I'm assuming we're going to remain discreet, correct?"

"If that's what you want."

She chewed on the corner of her lip. "If I

agree, I'd want it to be business as usual in the office, and when we're not at work, we can be like this."

"Like *this*?"

She rolled her eyes. "C'mon, Ronan, you know what I'm saying. Hawaii Ronan is very different than Bosshole Ronan."

I barked a laugh. "*Bosshole*, huh?"

She winced. "I didn't plan on *ever* saying that to your face. It just came out."

I hooked my foot around her ankle. "Is that what you call me behind my back?"

"That's what *everyone* at work calls you." I was fairly certain she was blushing. "Don't take this the wrong way, but you're not very likable, these last two days excluded. Respected, sure. Lusted after, definitely. But not liked."

My lip curled up in the corner. "You realize I couldn't care less, right? I'm there to make money, not friends. You're the first person in my thirteen years with the company that I ever wanted to be *friendly* with."

Quinn chuckled. "That's debatable."

"In all seriousness, I have to maintain a certain image in the office. When you're in my position, there's always someone waiting to shoot you down. If I give them 'Hawaii Ronan', it makes me vulnerable, and that's something that I'll never let happen.

You're the only person in that building who will ever see that side of me."

She looked at me thoughtfully. "And what makes me so special to have that honor?"

I smiled. "*Everything* makes you special, Quinn. Every-fucking-thing."

# CHAPTER NINETEEN

QUINN

"Mmm, this is the best dream."

Dream Ronan chuckled before flattening his tongue and licking me from bottom to top.

My back arched off the bed. "God, you're so good at that. Best. Pussy. Eater. Ever."

"I'm glad you approve," his deep voice rumbled against my hot flesh.

Wait a second...

My eyes snapped open in the darkened room. It took a moment for my brain to register where I was and what was happening. "Holy shit."

I wasn't dreaming. Ronan's dark head was actually moving between my legs. "Fuck, I could eat your pussy all day, every day. Breathing is overrated... I never want to come up for air."

"Yes, do that," I panted. "Never, *ever* stop doing this."

I couldn't stop squirming, so Ronan's heavy arm pinned me to the mattress as he continued licking and sucking, swirling his tongue or pressing the tip inside of me. My toes curled when his moans vibrated against my clit.

Before I knew it, my orgasm barreled down my spine and I was chanting his name over and over. He licked me slowly through the final tremor before kissing a path up my torso. The moonlight shone across his face as he hovered above me. "Hi there, beautiful."

"Hi, yourself. That was quite the morning wakeup call." I turned my head to check the time on the bedside table, seeing that it was just past two. "*Very* early morning."

He pulled my lower lip between his teeth before dipping his tongue into my mouth. I could taste my arousal on him and for some reason, I found it really sexy. I'd never been a big fan of kissing after oral, but with Ronan, it was hot. Everything about the man was a turn-on. My eyes rolled back as he teased me, sliding his cock back and forth over my swollen nub.

"I couldn't wait." Ronan cupped my breast, flicking his thumb over the stiff peak. We groaned in unison as he guided his length into my body with the other hand. "I can't get enough of you. I don't know if I'll *ever* get enough of you."

God, being with him like this was unreal. Skin to skin, the soft mattress at my back. Until the other night, I had never realized how I'd taken something like this for granted before. Don't get me wrong; sex with Ronan Maxwell was extraordinary, any location, in any position. But like this? Where it felt like we had all the time in the world... having him braced over me, where the scattering of coarse hair on his legs rubbed against the smoothness of mine, his fingers feathering over every inch of skin that he could reach? There was no better feeling on earth.

It was so perfect, it was terrifying.

I never expected him to bulldoze my walls so fast or so easily. This felt natural... like we'd always been this way. I couldn't help but wonder again what would happen when we returned to Los Angeles. When we got back to the real world, how would I reconcile the Ronan that lived in our little Hawaiian bubble, with the ruthless boss that I'd known for the last two years? I didn't know how I could go about my workday pretending I didn't know this other side of him.

He tucked his head into the crook of my neck. "Fuck, I love being inside of you. I love smelling like you afterward. All I think about lately is you. All I want is you."

My nails bit into his muscular ass as I pulled

him into me farther. "I can't think straight when you say things like that."

"So, stop thinking all the damn time. Just fucking *feel*." He thrust in and out a few times, driving my body insane with need.

I gasped when he hit that magical spot inside of me. "*Who are you? Ronan Maxwell overthinks everything.*"

His toothy smile gleamed in the moonlight. "Not like this. Not with you."

I whimpered as he bit down on the juncture of my neck and shoulder. "What does that even mean?"

He stilled as his large hands framed my face. "It means you're a game changer, Quinn. These last two days with you have been some of the best that I've had in a long fucking time. I don't want that to end. I don't want to go backward with you. I just want to fucking *be* with you."

"But—"

Ronan placed a gentle finger over my lips. "Shh. Let me finish. I know what I said on the plane. But I can't pretend I'd be okay if you walked away from this. I know our situation is complicated, but I think we can find a way to make it work. If you want to keep this quiet, I'm okay with that for now, as long as you give me all of you outside of the office. While we're at work, we'll keep it completely professional."

I gave him a wry look, even though he probably couldn't see it. "Because we've been so great at that already."

He chuckled. "I'm aware my self-control is shit around you, smartass. As is yours, I might add. But if we spent time together outside of the office, doing really fucking filthy things, I think that would help."

"I don't know, Ronan..."

"Shh... just *feel*."

His hands were seemingly everywhere at once —my hips, my thighs, my breasts, my face. He whispered in my ear, telling me how beautiful I was, how I was the smartest woman he'd ever met. How when we were together like this, nothing else mattered. Nothing else existed. I had never felt so close to another person than I did now. I no longer had any doubts about the power this man held over me. He could *eviscerate* me if he suddenly decided to change his mind. And as terrifying as that was, I found myself falling anyway, because how could I not? With his arms wrapped tightly around me, Ronan Maxwell did the one thing no man had done before. He made me feel hopeful for the future.

"Ugh, I don't wanna get up," I whined.

"So, go back to sleep." Ronan pulled me into him farther.

I wiggled my butt when he ground his erection into it. "It's rather hard with that thing knocking on my back door. How do I know you're not going to just try slipping it in?"

The rumble of his sleepy laughter did things to me. Sexy things. "Trust me, honey, back door access isn't something that can be done with any sort of stealth." The hand that was holding my breast moved south. "*When* I take your ass, we'll be doing lots of prep work before I try 'slipping it in'."

"So cocky. You're awfully confident that will happen."

He pressed into me. "I'll show you cocky."

"Oh, no, you won't." I wiggled out of his arms and slid off the bed. "Our flight to Maui leaves in three hours. I still have to pack and I'm guessing you do, too. We don't have time for all the sex."

"We can book a later flight."

"No can do, Bucko. Our first meeting is at noon."

He groaned. "You're such a buzzkill sometimes."

"Ha! Who would've ever thought *you'd* be saying that to *me*? Now, get out of here and pack your shit." I made a shooing gesture. "I'm taking a shower."

I had barely stepped under the spray of water

before I heard the bathroom door open. Ronan sauntered in, all toned and tan, and more importantly, naked. He stood just outside of the glass wall, with his large hand moving leisurely over his cock.

"What are you doing?"

He stepped behind the glass and leaned against the farthest wall of tiles. One of my favorite things about this hotel were the oversized showers. You could easily fit five people in here comfortably. Not that I was into orgies or anything.

Ronan gave himself one long stroke. "Watching you shower. Don't let me stop you. I'll just be right here doing my thing."

I couldn't take my eyes off of his hand, moving up and down over his length. His abs flexed when he grabbed his balls with the other hand and gave them a slight tug. Damn, that was hot. There was a high probability I was actually drooling right now.

"Quinn, didn't anyone ever teach you that it's rude to stare?"

My eyes snapped to his. "What?"

He chuckled and released his dick, much to my dismay. I watched as he grabbed my loofa, squirting a dollop of vanilla-scented body wash onto it and working it into a lather.

"Turn around. I'll wash your back."

We *really* didn't have time for this, but I found myself doing it anyway. He pushed my hair over my shoulder and peppered kisses down my neck. I groaned as he wrapped his hands around me, running the loofa over my sensitive breasts. After spending a great deal of time making sure they were extra clean, he moved the sponge lower. My hands flew to the wall for support as he ran it between my thighs, brushing over my clit just enough to feel good, but not enough to satisfy.

"Please," I whimpered. "Harder."

He dropped the loofa and started using his fingers to rub my hot flesh. One hand was anchored on my breast while the other teased me mercilessly. Every time I would get close, Ronan would back off completely.

"Still think we don't have enough time?" he murmured into my shoulder.

I stood on my toes as he rubbed faster, bringing me to the edge again. "Aaah, God, Ronan! Maybe just... maybe if we hurry."

I felt his smile against my skin. "Are you sure? Because if you're not, I can stop."

"Don't you dare!" I growled.

"Turn back around."

I didn't even hesitate because my need to come had overridden anything else.

Ronan dropped to the ground, putting him at eye level with my pussy. I didn't think I would ever get over the sight of this powerful, domineering man on his knees before me.

"Please," I repeated. "Put your mouth on me."

He spread my lower lips with his thumbs, blowing hot air over the spot where I wanted him most. His index finger ran down the middle, stopping when he reached my entrance.

"Mmm, we definitely don't have time for *that*. If I taste this pretty pussy right now, we'll never make it to the airport on time. You're going to have to settle for my hands this round."

"Fine... sure... do that. Just touch me, damn it."

"You're so fucking sexy when you get all bossy."

He resumed his sensual torture, working one, two, and then three fingers inside of me. It was sweet agony every time his thumb slid over my clit as he thrust his fingers upward. Finally—*God, finally*—he kept just enough pressure there to trigger my climax. It barreled out of me so fast, my knees buckled.

I pushed my wet hair back. "*Holy bejeezus.*"

Ronan placed a soft kiss on my thigh and stood up. "I'll take that as a compliment."

I gave him a lazy smile. "You should."

He stared at me intensely, tracing my jawline. "I'll step out and let you finish up."

I grabbed his forearm before he could walk away. "Wait. How quickly do you think you could come with my mouth?"

His wolfish grin sent a shiver through me. "*Very* quickly."

I chuckled. "Well, then sit your ass on that bench."

He made a show of sitting on the built-in bench and spreading his legs. "You don't need to tell me twice."

I lowered myself to the tiles and settled in between his thighs. His cock stood proud, resting over his belly button. I drew my tongue up the underside of his length, tracing the thick vein that ran down the center. Ronan groaned when I wrapped my lips around the flared head before releasing him and kissing down his length.

His fingers threaded through my hair. "Fuck, sweetheart. Don't tease me. I can't take it right now."

I hollowed my cheeks as I took him into my mouth, using my tongue along the way. His hips jerked, pushing him to the back of my throat.

Ronan grabbed a fistful of my hair. "Fuck, yeah, just like that."

I looked up as he gathered my hair to the side so he could watch. I swore his cock grew bigger once our gazes met. I focused on fighting my gag reflex as I sucked harder, moving up and down his shaft. He started moving his hips faster, fucking my mouth as if he just couldn't help himself.

"Christ, you're so pretty with your mouth wrapped around my dick."

I hummed around him as we fell into a rhythm

of sorts. My mouth and fist worked in tandem with his hips. Ronan's choppy breaths and mumbled praise spurred me on. I got lost in the moment, sucking him in earnest, listening to his cues. He traced the indentation of my cheek with his finger, keeping the other hand firmly glued to the back of my head, holding my hair away.

"Fuck, Quinn. I'm going to come."

I moaned as his abs flexed and his thighs tensed. I increased the suction as he surged into my mouth, pulling in slow drags as he rode out the high. When he finished, I pulled away and sat back with a smile, Ronan's salty taste coating my tongue.

"Is there anything you can't do? That was the best blow job I've ever had." His head fell back. "Jesus *fuck*."

While I didn't like to think of him with other women, his comment filled me with a sense of pride. Before I knew what was happening, Ronan had reversed our positions.

"What are you doing?" I asked.

He pulled my legs over his shoulders and spread me wide. "Returning the favor."

"Ronan..." My voice drifted off as he gave me one long lick down the center. "We... don't... have... time."

He hummed as he swirled his tongue around. "I don't fucking care."

# CHAPTER TWENTY

**RONAN**

"I think this is my new favorite place in the whole world."

I hummed in agreement as I stroked Quinn's back. After touring the Maui property, we hit up the activities concierge for a paddleboard. Now, with me flat on my back, and Quinn's body stretched over mine, we were floating on the board over the clear, turquoise waters of Honokeana Bay.

She lifted her head slightly. "So, this is one of your favorite places on the island?"

I skated my fingers over the warm water. "It is. In the winter, it's a great place to surf if you go out a little deeper. The rest of the year, the water's nice and still, so I'll usually go snorkeling or paddle-boarding. Plus, since this is a residential area, it's usually pretty empty."

Her coffee-colored eyes widened. "You *surf?*"

I nodded. "Since I was ten years old. Back home, I'm in the ocean almost every weekend. It recharges me for the upcoming workweek."

She shook her head. "Seriously, *who are you?*"

I grinned. "I'm the same man I've always been. I'm just letting you see all of me now."

Quinn ran her delicate fingers over my jaw. "I *really* like all of you."

"I *really* like all of you, too." I grabbed her ass. "Especially this part."

"Oh, God, you just had to go and ruin it, didn't you?" The sparkle in her eyes told me she didn't really mean that. She gasped when a sea turtle swam to the surface right beside us. "I can't believe how many turtles there are."

"They're always here. I think they like the protection the cove offers them."

Quinn rested her head against my chest again, turning her face toward the neighboring islands off in the distance. "It's so peaceful here."

My fingers glided down her arm. "Just wait until you see where I'm taking you tomorrow. You'll never want to leave."

"I'm already feeling like that. I'm so glad you wanted to book the extra days." She sighed and squeezed me around the middle. "The sun will be setting soon. We should probably head back."

"You feel like grabbing some food?" I tapped her back, prompting her to sit up.

Quinn sat on her knees while I moved to the front of the board, careful not to flip us. "Mmm, I could go for some food."

I dipped the paddle in the water and began steering us ashore. "There's this really great taco place right here in Napili. You in?"

"You had me at taco."

"Noted. The girl likes tacos."

I could hear the smile in her voice. "I couldn't be friends with someone who didn't like tacos."

"Is that what we are? *Friends?*"

Quinn cleared her throat. "I don't know, Ronan. To me, this feels like a lot more than friends. Am I reading things wrong?"

I glanced back with a wink. "No, sweetheart, I think you're reading things just right."

The next morning, we were awoken by the shrill ringtone of my phone. I let it go to voicemail, but then it started all over again.

"Make it stop," Quinn groaned.

I fumbled for my cell sitting on the nightstand. Once I saw that my COO was calling, I answered immediately. He would never call me unless it was absolutely necessary.

"Yes, Mr. Moore, what can I do for you?"

"Mr. Maxwell," he said quickly. "Sir, I know you're in Hawaii, but I think you need to return to the office immediately."

Well, now I was perfectly alert. The tone in his voice told me that I wasn't going to like what he was about to say. Quinn looked at me questioningly when I sat up abruptly, but my attention was on the phone line.

"What happened?"

He released a heavy sigh. "Sir, the FBI is here. They showed up with a warrant about ten minutes ago. They took Mr. Landers into custody and they're ransacking his office."

What. The. Fuck.

Henry Landers was my Chief Financial Officer. Whatever the hell was going on, it wasn't good.

I rolled my neck from side to side, trying to release some of the tension. "Why?"

"I don't know, sir. The legal department is trying to get information now."

Fuck. If the feds were in my office, arresting one of my executives, I knew that pure chaos was close behind. I got out of bed and immediately started throwing shit into my suitcase. Quinn and I had kept the second reserved room for appearances, but we'd been staying in the same one.

"Listen to me. Don't say a word to anyone. Instruct the staff not to say a word to anyone. I will be there as soon as possible. I'll call my brother and get his team over there to coach everyone. I don't know how soon I can get a flight out, but the flight time alone is five hours. I'll update you when I get more information."

"Yes, sir."

I pressed the end button on my phone and faced Quinn. She had her laptop at the ready, already surmising that shit was hitting the fan.

"What's going on?" she asked.

"I need to get back to L.A. right away. I don't know what's happening exactly, but the FBI just arrested my goddamn CFO and they're going through his office."

Her eyes widened. "Oh shit."

I scrubbed my hands over my face. "Exactly."

Quinn started typing furiously. "I'll book us the first flight out."

"No, don't do that—just book one for me. You stay here. Enjoy the next two days. I'll leave the Jeep so you can explore the island a bit."

She shook her head. "Ronan, no way. You're going to need help. That's my job."

"Normally, yes, but I have a feeling there's nothing anyone can do right now but wait for more information and try to keep this out of the media. It's only two days. I can manage."

"But—"

"Quinn, I don't want to argue with you about

this. Take the time off—there's no sense in both of us missing out. The only thing I need from you is a booked flight."

She nodded. "Okay... if you're sure."

"I'm sure." I pulled on my pants and dialed my brother's number.

Liam answered on the first ring. "Ro, what's up?"

"I need you to head to my office now. Drop whatever the fuck you have going on—there's a storm brewing."

"What? I thought you were in Hawaii."

"I am, but I'm taking the first flight back. I'll call you with details when I'm on my way to the airport. Just get over there."

"I'm on it."

Quinn ended the call she was on at the same time. "I called the concierge. He's securing a town car for you. It should be pulling up by the time you get down there." She turned back to her computer. "We're in luck. There's a flight leaving in just over two hours. The drive to the airport will take about forty-five minutes, so you'll need to haul ass, but you should be able to make it. Unless you need it, don't worry about your luggage. I'll bring it back with me."

I finished buttoning my shirt and grabbed a tie. I knew I'd have to go straight to headquarters, so there was no sense in dressing down. "That'd be great."

I took a moment to appreciate the fact that she was still completely naked. Quinn had slipped into business mode seamlessly, but she didn't bother dressing. Damn, I wished I had time to do something about it.

She chewed on her lower lip when she saw the undoubtedly hungry look in my eyes. "Are you sure you don't want me to come?"

"I'm positive. Enjoy the next two days and I'll see you back home." I knelt down on the mattress and pulled her into a kiss. "But if you do feel the need to *come*, make sure you think of me."

Her beautiful face lit up with a smile as she covered herself with the sheet. "If you're lucky, maybe I'll even send you pictures."

I grabbed my laptop bag and pulled the door open. "Yes, do that. *Definitely* do that."

"Text me when you land or call if you need anything." She blew me a kiss.

I winked and stepped into the hallway, closing the door behind me.

After what felt like the longest flight in history, I finally made it back to headquarters. Using the plane's Wi-Fi, I was able to keep in constant contact with them, but it made me anxious not being there in person. So far, we knew that the feds were pressing charges against my CFO for insider trading. I didn't know what those charges entailed, but the accusation alone was bad enough.

Henry Landers had been with the company for over twenty years. He was well respected in the industry—I couldn't imagine him doing something like this, but I knew the Securities & Exchange Commission didn't make these accusations without just cause. There would've been a thorough investigation before the FBI stepped in to make an arrest.

"What do you have?" I'd texted Liam as I entered the building, so he was waiting for me as I stepped off the elevator.

He followed me to my office. "Well, I'm guessing you saw the vultures camped out in front of the building. Suffice it to say, the press is going nuts. They're asking for a statement, which I've already drafted and sent to your email. Just thought you'd want to take a look before it became public."

I powered up my computer and took a seat. My inbox was flooded with messages that had already been flagged and color coded in order of importance. Quinn was the only other person who had access to my email, so she'd obviously been working while I was in the air. I opened our interoffice communication system and could see she was still online, so I sent her a message.

*Ronan Maxwell, CEO: Do I need to have IT suspend your system access? I told you to take time off.*

*Quinn Montgomery, Executive Assistant to the CEO: I*

*can't help it. It's driving me crazy that I'm not with you. Any updates?*

*Ronan Maxwell, CEO: Even if I had any, I wouldn't give them to you because you should be TAKING TIME OFF.*

*Quinn Montgomery, Executive Assistant to the CEO: Ronan, stop being so difficult. I know you're stressed out. Let me help.*

*Ronan Maxwell, CEO: If you want to help alleviate my stress, go take some of those pictures you mentioned earlier. I wasn't joking about calling IT. If I see you online again, consider it done.*

*Quinn Montgomery, Executive Assistant to the CEO: Stubborn ass.*

*Ronan Maxwell, CEO: You love it.*

*Quinn Montgomery, Executive Assistant to the CEO: Not at the moment. \*Zany face emoji \*Zany face emoji*

*Ronan Maxwell, CEO: Close your computer and get to work on those pictures. Remember, I don't make empty threats.*

*Quinn Montgomery, Executive Assistant to the CEO: I'm glaring at you right now.*

I laughed as I typed my reply.

*Ronan Maxwell, CEO: I'll call you as soon as I can. XO*

I composed an email to IT, knowing she wouldn't listen to me. After I hit send, I looked up and found my brother smiling like he was sitting on a juicy secret.

"What are you so smiley about?"

"I could ask you the same. Considering the current circumstances, you must've been talking to someone pretty special." He looked around. "Speaking of *pretty special someones...* where is your beautiful assistant?"

I narrowed my eyes. "Maui. Why do you care?"

"Why didn't she come back with you?"

"Because I told her to take a couple of days off," I answered matter-of-factly. "She's never been to Maui before—I wanted her to enjoy it. There's not much she can do anyway until we figure out what's going on."

Liam's eyes lit up with amusement. "Interesting."

"What the fuck are you talking about?"

He laughed. "Are you still going to lie to my face and tell me you're not fucking her?"

I rubbed my temples. "Jesus, Liam, not this again. We have other shit to worry about right now."

"So, you *are* fucking her. Glad we finally got that out of the way." Liam held his hands up when I glared at him. "Hey man, I'm the last person who would judge you. Quinn's brilliant, driven, and fucking gorgeous. Quite frankly, I'm surprised it took you this long. I only made it six months with Avery before I snapped."

"I'm not just fucking her," I growled.

He steepled his fingers. "No? Then what *are* you doing with your lovely assistant?"

I rolled a pen back and forth over my desk. Fuck it, if anyone could keep a secret, it was this man. "I... want to be with her. With or without the fucking. I really like being around her, whatever the reason."

Liam smiled. "It's about damn time you admitted that. Does she know?"

"Yes, she knows. She feels the same. Now can we move past all this feelings bullshit and—"

"Ronan," a familiar voice called. "Liam."

My father was standing in the open doorway, looking displeased. *How long had he been there?*

"Dad! What are you doing here?" I rounded my desk and sat on the edge.

Liam stood as well. "Hey, Dad."

The slight wrinkles on my father's face deepened when he frowned. "I saw the news. What the hell is going on with Hank?"

"I don't know yet. We're waiting to hear back from Legal whether or not the charges will stick."

"Insider trading, Ronan?" he shouted. "Do you have any idea what this can do to the company?"

Christ, this was the last thing I needed. I loved my father, and I respected the hell out of him, but he was a difficult man to *like*. I frowned when I realized that Quinn had described my work personality in an eerily similar manner.

"I am well aware of the possible ramifications." I clenched my jaw. "In case you forgot, *I* am the CEO now. I have it handled."

"Do you?" he challenged. "Because to me, it sounds like your head is so far up your EA's skirt, that you haven't been paying attention to what matters. You and your brother are sitting here talking about your goddamn *feelings* like a couple of teenage girls, instead of taking action to squash the speculation! Our stock is plummeting!"

Liam coughed into his fist. "Yeah... I'm going to leave you two alone. I have a statement to release."

I waited until my brother had shut the door behind him. "Dad, how in the hell was I supposed to know this was going to happen? Henry Landers has been an outstanding employee for over two decades. One that *you* hired."

My father's eyes, identical to my own, narrowed into slits. "Did you know that his wife left him? *For the goddamn lawn boy?* And she's trying to take him for all he's worth?"

I tugged on my hair. "What does *that* have to do with our current situation? And why the hell do *you* know that?"

"Because while I was running this ship, I was very good at the one thing you're not: getting to know my employees. Hank and I went golfing just last month."

"Again, what does *that* have to do with our current situation? I'm not here to make friends."

He scoffed. "I didn't say you needed to make friends, but it wouldn't kill you to ask about their personal lives every now and again. If you get to know your employees, you learn their mannerisms. You know what's going on in their world outside of this building. You'd have a much better chance of knowing if something wasn't right. If you weren't so busy screwing some career-climbing bimbo, maybe you would've known what Hank was up to. For all we know, he was so desperate, he felt like he had no other choice."

I clenched my fists, resisting the urge to punch the man. "Quinn is *not* a career-climbing bimbo. Leave her out of this. This has nothing to do with her."

"Really?" My father smiled coldly. "You can honestly tell me that she doesn't distract you from doing your job? That she doesn't... oh, let's say, suddenly spend an inordinate amount of time with you locked in your office? That you haven't repeatedly cleared your schedule, pushing off important meetings? Can you refute *any* of that?"

"*What the fuck?* Do you have goddamn spies in this building or something?"

"I have eyes *everywhere*, Ronan! And they've all said the same thing—that you've been *off* lately. Distracted by goddamn pussy! If you two thought you were being discreet, that's just another example of how far removed you've become." His face was so red, it was turning purple. "*Fix this.* I don't care how the fuck you manage that, but you'd better fix this. Don't make me use my considerable influence with the board to take away the position you supposedly love." With that, he stormed out of my office.

I slammed my balled fists on my desk. "*Fuck!*"

I'd hate to admit that my father was right, but facts were facts. I *had* been distracted lately. And the cause of that distraction was one-hundred percent Quinn Montgomery.

# CHAPTER TWENTY-ONE

QUINN

"Oh my God, girl, I have been trying to reach you for hours!"

I held my hand up, stopping Antonio from saying another word. "Slow down there, buddy. I just stepped off the elevator."

He propped his hand on his hip, cocking his head. "Why the hell haven't you been answering my texts? I know you were on a plane, but I *also* know they have Wi-Fi. Why are you avoiding me? I need to know what happened in Hawaii."

My brows pinched together. "What are you talking about?"

"You're finally here!" Sylvie power-walked down the hall until she stood directly in front of me. "Why the hell aren't you answering your phone?"

"Jeez, you guys, calm down. I accidentally left

my charger at the hotel and didn't realize it until we were already in the air. My phone died about thirty minutes into the flight." I started walking toward my office, rolling Ronan's suitcase behind me. "Now, what's the big deal? Is this about Mr. Landers?"

Antonio tugged on my elbow right outside my office. "Stop walking. What the hell happened between you and Mr. Maxwell in Hawaii?"

Holy crap, had Ronan said something about our new relationship? No, that just wasn't possible, given his stance on keeping his personal life private.

"I'm going to need you to elaborate on that," I said as I turned the handle to my door.

Sylvie grabbed me this time. "Quinn, wait. Don't—"

When I stepped into my office, I had to look back and check the nameplate. Ronan's name was still on the door, but for some reason, our COO's assistant, Ms. Stuart, was sitting behind my desk. Was she acting as his temp in my absence?

She pushed her glasses up the bridge of her nose. "May I help you with something, Miss Montgomery?"

"Um... no, thank you. I appreciate you filling in for me, but I'm back so you can return to Mr. Moore now."

She appraised me thoughtfully. "Miss Montgomery, I'm afraid you're mistaken. *You* now report to Mr. Moore. There was a company-wide memo a few hours ago. I'm guessing you haven't had a chance to read it?"

*What the hell?*

"No, I haven't had the chance to read anything because my system access has been blocked for the last few days!"

She narrowed her eyes at me. "There's no need to shout."

I looked back to Antonio and Sylvie. "Did you guys know about this?"

Antonio threw his hands up. "Yes! That's what we were trying to talk to you about."

"This has to be a mistake." I headed toward Ronan's office and reached for the handle.

Ms. Stuart jumped up from the desk. "You can't just go in there! He's very busy."

The door was locked, so I pounded on it with my fist. "Mr. Maxwell, I need a moment of your time. There seems to be some sort of mix-up."

I pounded three more times before the door was yanked open. Ronan surveyed the room, taking note of our audience, before addressing me calmly. "Miss Montgomery, what can I do for you?"

My mouth fell open. "Ms. Stuart seems to think she is reporting to you now, and *I* am reporting to Mr. Moore. Please tell her she's mistaken."

His unshaven jaw ticked. "I'm afraid *you're* the one who's mistaken, Miss Montgomery. Since you obviously didn't get the memo, please step inside my office and I will explain." He looked up. "Everyone else, get back to work."

Ms. Stuart huffed and returned to her chair —*my* chair—and Sylvie mouthed *good luck* as she and Antonio fled the scene.

Ronan stepped aside so I could walk in and he grabbed his suitcase before closing the door behind me. "Miss Montgomery, if you'll—"

"Would you stop with the Miss Montgomery crap?" I whispered harshly. "There's nobody else here."

He cleared his throat. "Miss Montgomery, as I was saying, I—"

"Ronan, what the hell is wrong with you?! Why haven't you been answering my texts? I know you've been busy, but—"

"If you let me get a damn word in edgewise, I could explain," he snapped. "Now, have a damn seat."

I folded my arms over my chest. "I'd rather stand. At least until you tell me what the fuck is going on."

He draped himself into his chair as if he didn't have a care in the world. "As I was saying... I decided that it was time to move you to another area of the company. In order to grow within the company, you need to—"

"*Move me to ano—*"

Ronan held his hand up. "Let me finish, for fuck's sake!"

I gestured for him to take the floor. "By all means. This should be good."

He straightened his tie. "As I was saying—and I swear to Christ, if you interrupt me again, I will flip the fuck out—I decided it was best to transfer you to a different area of business. Maxwell Hotels values you as an employee and we want to foster an environment where continued growth can be achieved. It's a lateral move; your salary and title will not change—only who you're reporting to. This move will allow you to learn more about the operational side of this business."

"That's bullshit, Ronan! What's the real reason? You don't think I should report to you any longer because of our personal relationship?"

He stretched his neck to the side. "I'm afraid you're mistaken there as well, Miss Montgomery. We do not *have* a personal relationship."

I blinked a few times to make sure I wasn't hallucinating. "I'm sorry, *what*? What about everything that happened in Hawaii?"

Ronan loosened his tie and popped the first button on his shirt open. "Surely, you don't think I should be held accountable for anything I said during pillow talk?" He gave me a slimy grin. "Miss Montgomery, your pussy is truly exceptional, and I enjoyed our time together, but that's run its course now, don't you think? I trust that you will remain professional and not breathe a word about our sexual encounters to anyone."

"Wow... I don't know what the fuck to say to that." I pinched the bridge of my nose to fight off the looming tears. "So... to be clear, when you said you wanted to be with me on a personal level, you didn't mean a word of it? It was all just 'pillow talk' that I shouldn't take seriously?"

He swallowed. "That's exactly what I'm saying. I'm glad we're both in agreement. Now if you'll excu—"

I held my hand up to cut him off. "Stop. Just *fucking stop lying to me!* If you can't be man enough to tell me the truth, then *fuck you*, Ronan. Fuck you *and* your lateral move bullshit. You don't need to worry about my professionalism—or lack thereof— because I *quit*."

If I wasn't mistaken, I'd swear he looked upset, but that was quickly masked.

"You're being childish, don't you think?" He couldn't possibly have looked more bored as he said that. "You and I both know that you won't find a better opportunity than what you have here. Or a better salary. Quite frankly, Miss Montgomery, you're crazy if you think leaving is the best answer."

I laughed, a little maniacally if I was being honest. "You know what? Maybe I *am* crazy considering how many stupid, reckless decisions I've made over the last month. But don't worry; I'm seeing things perfectly clear now. I couldn't be more confident that leaving is the best solution. I've put up with you for two years too long and I'm not going to waste another minute of my life doing it." I walked across the room and opened the door. Before leaving, I turned back and said, "*Fuck you*, Ronan. I'm sorry I ever met you."

I barely made it to the elevator before the tears burst loose.

"Oh, honey, I'm so sorry." Sylvie rubbed my back soothingly.

I took a gulp of wine. I should probably stop soon, but this situation called for copious amounts of wine and chocolate. Sylvie and Antonio, being the wonderful friends they were, showed up on my doorstep with plenty of both. For the last thirty minutes, the three of us had been sitting on my couch while I'd given them the recap.

"I can't believe I was so stupid. He seemed so genuine, but it was all a game to him. I knew he was a bastard, but I had no idea he was capable of being so *cruel*."

Antonio pulled me into a side hug. "Oh, babe, I don't think any of us did."

I sniffled. "Thank you, guys, for bringing my

stuff. I can't imagine how awful it would've been having to go back there to get it."

Yet another reason I was so lucky to have them. When Antonio saw me practically running out of the office, he knew something bad had happened.

Sylvie refilled our glasses. "I still can't believe he did that to you. It doesn't make any sense. After two years of employment, why now? If this was just some sort of sick mind game to him, why now? And why you? You're the one person who makes his life easier at work and the only one who's put up with him longer than a few months. I just don't get it."

"Probably because he knew I wouldn't cry sexual harassment," I mumbled. "I own up to my mistakes. I would never play the victim card just because I can't accept responsibility for my actions. I'm sure he could sense how attracted I was to him —he knew I'd enthusiastically jump into bed with him."

Antonio shook his head. "It still doesn't make sense. That man could snap his fingers and beautiful women would come running."

"It doesn't matter if it makes sense or not. Whatever the reason, he played me. I *knew* getting involved with him was a bad idea, but I did it anyway." I hung my head in my hands and groaned. "God, I'm such a fucking idiot."

"Oh sweetie, no, you're not," Sylvie argued. "You're human."

"We should quit too," Antonio suggested. "That asshole will see how good he had it when he can't find people who can do the job half as well as we can."

I shook my head. "Don't even think about it. It's an amazing company to work for and you guys have seniority. Besides, he knows how close we are. If you quit too, he'd know how badly I'm hurting and that's the last thing I'd want. I may feel like shit now, but I'll find a way to get over it. I don't want to give him the satisfaction of knowing how much he got to me."

Sylvie sighed. "So, what do you think you're going to do? For work, I mean."

I shrugged. "I don't know. I'd really like to stay in the hotel industry if I can. I suppose I'll give the headhunter HR uses a call. Maybe she knows of some openings."

"And what about Ronan Maxwell?" Antonio bumped his shoulder against mine. "What are you going to do about him? You already have a revenge body—how do you plan on showing him what he's missing out on?"

"I don't," I sighed. "As far as Ronan Maxwell is concerned, I just hope I can get shitfaced enough tonight to forget he was ever a part of my life."

Sylvie grabbed the box of gourmet chocolates and held it out for me. "We love you, Quinnie. We're here for whatever you need."

I selected a coconut truffle. "I love you guys, too. I don't know what I'd do without you."

"Good thing you're never getting rid of us," Antonio said and winked, making me laugh for the first time today.

I knew it would take some time, but I was determined to get over Ronan Maxwell. I just needed to figure out how.

# CHAPTER TWENTY-TWO

**RONAN**

It'd been two weeks since I'd made the biggest mistake of my life. I was so fucking ashamed of myself for letting my father get to me—for allowing his threat to take root. For *crushing* the woman that I'd loved. What good was doing what I loved for a living if I didn't have her by my side? I was fucking miserable without Quinn. It was a classic case of not knowing what you had until it was gone. I knew that I had feelings for her, but I hadn't realized the depth of those feelings until she walked out of my life. Or, before I forced her out, rather.

Fuck.

As for my business, it was like the whole insider trading incident never happened, despite the fact that my former CFO was awaiting trial. All thanks to my brother, the master publicist. He managed to spin the story with such finesse, the press quickly lost interest. I knew that wouldn't be the case once the trial started, but at least Liam had a head's up this time. For now, my board was happy, our stock was up, and everything around the office was status quo. I should've been happy, right? But happy was the complete opposite of what I was feeling.

I took a sip of cheap whiskey and relished the burn. I didn't deserve top shelf liquor after what I had done. There wasn't a minute that went by when I didn't wonder how Quinn was doing. When I didn't want to go to her house and beg for forgiveness. I had tried calling her and found her number had been disconnected. It was pretty obvious she wanted nothing to do with me.

"Buy me a drink?"

I glanced at the woman who sidled up next to me. I motioned for the bartender to take her order.

She smiled as she picked up the wine glass. "I'm Cassie. And you are?"

"Enjoy your drink, Cassie." I nodded and turned away from her.

"Seriously?" she huffed.

I took a deep breath before turning back in her direction. "Look, I'm sure you're a lovely woman, but I'm not interested."

"Asshole," she muttered as she stomped away.

"Tell me about it."

"Damn, that's the tenth woman I've watched

you turn down over the last two weeks." The bartender set another drink in front of me. "Every night, you come in here, order shit alcohol—despite the fact that I *know* you can afford better, considering you own the building across the street. So, in my experience, if you're in here trying to get drunk instead of laid, that means you're trying to *get over* a woman. You want to talk about it?"

I shook my head. "Not really."

He laughed. "Okay, man, I get the hint. If you change your mind, let me know."

I nodded and resumed drowning my sorrows.

A short while later, another woman approached me. I knew this particular woman had no interest in hitting on me though. If anything, she'd rather cut off my dick.

Sylvie O'Hare took the seat beside me and glared. "You're a real asshole, you know that?"

I gave her a wry look. "I'm well aware."

"Yeah?" She raised her carefully sculpted brows. "Well, were you *aware* that she's leaving?"

We both knew to whom she was referring, so I didn't even pretend otherwise. "What do you mean, she's *leaving*? She already *left*."

Miss O'Hare shook her head. "She's *moving*, you jackass."

I narrowed my eyes. "Watch it. I'm still your boss."

"I'll risk it." She rolled her eyes. "My best friend

is about to pick up and leave everything she's ever known. The same woman who gets cold when the temperature drops below sixty, is going to move to *Chicago*—a place that might as well be Antarctica in the winter—because she so adamantly insists on staying in the hotel industry."

"There are plenty of hotels in California."

"There are," she agreed. "But she was offered a job with Onyx Hotels and they're headquartered in Chicago. Do you want to know what position they're giving her?"

I took another sip of my drink. "I'm sure you're about to tell me."

"*An intern!*"

My jaw clenched. "Why *the fuck* would she accept that?"

Miss O'Hare threw her hands up. "Oh, I don't know... maybe because her heart is so broken, she felt like she had to get the hell out of Dodge? That was the first offer she received, and she jumped on it, despite the fact that she's going to be overqualified and underpaid." She stabbed me in the chest with her finger. "She loved you and you fucked up, buddy."

"I know." I finished the remainder of my whiskey. "But this is none of your business."

She scoffed. "Well, too bad, because I'm *making it* my business. Quinn would *kill me* if she knew I was here right now. I'm risking losing her trust by talking to you. You wanna know why?"

"I'm guessing you'll tell me regardless of my answer, so go ahead."

Miss O'Hare stabbed me in the chest again. "Because I think you love her too, if the fact that you've been moping around like a sad sack of shit is any indication. I don't know why you did what you did, but I do think there was a reason at the time. Not a *good* reason, but a reason nonetheless."

I ground my teeth together, trying to calm down. "When does she leave?"

"Two weeks from today," she answered. "Don't take too long to think about it because if she actually goes through with this... if she moves *two thousand miles away*, she'll likely stick with it no matter how unhappy it makes her. You know how fiercely loyal she is. I really don't want to see my best friend living a lie, so you need to pull up your big boy undies and beg for her forgiveness. The question is, are you man enough to do whatever it takes to get your girl back?"

I didn't think arriving half-drunk was a good idea, so I waited until the next morning to make my move. Now, I was standing on Quinn's front porch, waiting for her to let me in. I'd rang the doorbell twice *and* knocked, but she wasn't coming to the door. I knew she was most likely home because her Audi was parked in the driveway. Odds were, she was simply hoping I'd go away if she ignored me long enough.

I knocked again. "I know you're there, Quinn. If you're not ready to open the door, I'll just wait here until you are."

I heard someone moving inside the house, getting closer. I knew it was her—my heart was trying to beat its way out of my chest to run to her. "Please go away, Ronan. I have nothing to say to you."

I pressed my forehead against the wood. "Quinn, please, just give me five minutes. Baby, I'm so sorry. I didn't mean a word of it and I'd like the chance to explain what happened. I know I don't deserve it after the way I treated you, but *please*, just give me five minutes."

The silence on the other end was deafening. As she unlatched the lock however many minutes later, I breathed a sigh of relief, but then my chest ached when I got my first glimpse of her. Quinn's eyes were puffy and red-rimmed, the gold flecks in them much brighter than usual. A dozen emotions flashed across her face at once—anger, sadness, and uncertainty, to name a few. I hated that I was the cause of her distress. I wanted so desperately to pull her into my arms, telling her that it would be okay.

That I would find a way to make it work. I knew I had several hoops to jump through before that would even be a possibility though.

"Ronan, I really don't want to do this. I think you've said enough already."

I stuck my foot in the doorway when she tried closing it. "Quinn, please. I promise you can tell me to fuck off if you want after I'm done, but I need to say this, and I really don't think your neighbors need to witness it." I looked around to emphasize my point. The neighbors on each side of her were gardening, hearing every word we were saying.

She sighed as she stepped aside. "Five minutes and not a second more."

Since I was on the clock, I decided not to waste time by beating around the bush. "I'm so sorry, Quinn. I've never been sorrier for anything in my life. I know I don't deserve it, but I'm begging you to hear me out."

Quinn shook her head as her eyes filled with tears. "Why should I? What good are words if you can just take them back?"

I winced. "I deserved that. If you still want me out of your life after I'm done, I'll go. Please, I just need you to *listen*."

She glared. "Fine. Talk."

"I know you're angry, as you should be. And I know you're hurt, but there's a reason why I said those horrible things to you."

Her fists clenched at her side. "Don't assume to know what I'm thinking or feeling. You don't know me."

I held my hands up. "I beg to differ, but that's a conversation for another time."

"Assuming there will *be* another time," she scoffed.

I continued, despite her jab. "When I got back from Maui, my father paid me a visit."

She frowned. "So?"

"So... he said some things. He knew about us—I don't know who his source is, but he obviously has someone feeding him information."

Her jaw dropped. "How could that be? We were careful not to get caught."

I shrugged. "Not careful enough, apparently. He accused me of being distracted... that maybe if I wasn't so consumed by you, I would've known something was off with Henry Landers. That maybe I could've somehow prevented this. He made a pretty convincing argument."

Quinn rolled her eyes. "That's a bunch of crap. The odds of that are so low, it's ridiculous to even think it."

I gave her a sad smile. "I know that, *now*. But at the time... there was so much going on at once, I didn't... I guess you could say I was blinded by the need for my father's approval. I know he can be an asshole, but he was always a brilliant businessman. If he approved of how I was running the company, I knew I was on the right track. Conversely, if he didn't... well, that's what led to my decision to shut you out. Plus, he threatened to petition the board, calling for my termination, if I didn't clean up the mess as fast as possible."

"He can't do that."

I shook my head. "The hell he can't. They take every word that leaves his mouth as scripture. He may be retired, but he's never truly left the company. You know that, Quinn."

She lowered her gaze. "It doesn't matter, Ronan. You could've just told me this—we could've figured it out together. But instead, you made the choice to push me out of your life, in *the cruelest way possible*."

"I know, but—"

She held her hand up. "There's nothing more to say."

*The fuck there wasn't.*

"Don't go to Chicago."

Her eyes widened. "How do you know about Chicago?"

Shit. I didn't think about that part. I didn't want to get her friend in trouble, but how else could I explain it?

"Does it matter?" I hedged. "What matters is that you *shouldn't go*. You'd be miserable. Onyx's

CEO is an even bigger prick than I am, and your talent would be wasted there! *Don't* go."

She shook her head. "You don't get a say in the matter."

"Look, I know I don't, but..." I reached for her but thought better of it when she flinched. "Can you honestly say that you'd be happy there? There's no ocean. It's below freezing during the winter. Your best friends live *here*. Your parents live *here*. Take me completely out of the equation and name one good reason why you should move there."

Quinn nibbled her lip, like she always did when she was deep in thought. "Because... it's time to make a fresh start and I can't do that here."

"You want a fresh start? Fine. Come work in finance. We have an opening and it's completely different from what you've been doing."

Her jaw dropped. "You're joking, right? I can't go back there. Nobody would take me seriously— especially now that people know that we were... sleeping together."

"That's bullshit," I argued. "Anyone can see how damn competent you are and that's all that matters. Nobody would question why you got the job. You're a goddamn genius with numbers. Literally! Anyone who can't see that can fuck off."

"You don't get it, Ronan. They wouldn't question *you*, but I don't have that luxury."

"That's not true and you know it. You know

*more than anyone* how hard I work to prove myself daily and you know exactly why. Fuck, we were just talking about it two minutes ago!" I ran my hands through my hair. "You don't want the finance job, fine. Come back to your old position. Just come back to *me*."

Her tears fell freely now. "I can't."

"Why the hell not?"

She looked me right in the eye as she stabbed me in the heart. "Because I don't trust you."

"Quinn, I—"

She wiped tears away as she made her way to the door. As she opened it, she said, "Please, just go, Ronan. If you ever had any real feelings for me, you wouldn't fight me on this."

I stepped outside, trying to think of a way to get through to her. There was only one thing I could think of that might work. This wasn't how I'd wanted to tell her, but desperate times called for desperate measures.

"I love you, Quinn. I don't want to be without you. Please, just give me a chance to prove it."

Her eyes shot to mine. "Actions speak louder than words, Ronan. If you truly *love me*, then respect my wishes and walk away. I don't want you in my life anymore."

Well, fuck.

# CHAPTER TWENTY-THREE

QUINN

"I can't believe you're leaving!" Antonio cried.

"Me neither." Sylvie sniffled as she pulled me into a hug. "Bitch, you'd better Skype us all the time."

"I will. I promise."

They both insisted on driving me to the airport and following me inside, dragging out our goodbyes as long as possible. Since I didn't know when I'd be able to see them next, I was soaking it up.

Sylvie dabbed at her tears. "Don't worry about the house. We'll try not to break anything."

I chuckled. "Thank you."

I had decided to keep my house as a rental, but with only two weeks to prepare for my move, I hadn't had much time to pack. I'd hired a property management firm to deal with tenants and such, but I still had a bunch of personal belongings that I needed to clear out. Since I didn't have a permanent place in Chicago yet, I decided to put my things into storage for now, which Antonio and Sylvie so graciously insisted on doing for me. Once I found an apartment, I could hire movers to bring everything to me.

Antonio hugged me once more but didn't let go when he pulled back. "Have you heard from him?"

I shook my head. "No. He's honoring my wishes."

He gave me a sad smile. "It's not too late, you know. He's miserable without you—he's not even trying to hide it these days. Do you know he's gone through *fifteen* temps in the month that you've been gone? He's even asked about you, like he's willing to eat any morsel that I throw at him. It's gotta be *killing him* that he has to resort to that."

It was practically killing *me* being away from him. I felt like I couldn't breathe anytime I thought about Ronan, which was pretty much all the time. I couldn't stop replaying his words, wondering if he'd spoken the truth. Deep down, I knew he meant them—you couldn't fake the connection we had—but that didn't erase all the pain that he'd caused.

I swallowed the lump in my throat. "It *is* too late. I don't know if I can ever forgive him and I can't be here when everything reminds me of us. I need a fresh start." I checked the time on my phone. "I need to get to my gate. They're boarding in ten minutes. I love you guys."

"Love you," they both said in unison.

During the flight, I tried thinking of anything but Ronan but failed miserably. I was reading a book by Julia Wolf, which probably made matters worse, but I was so sucked into it, I couldn't stop. The woman in the story took a summer job working for a rock star. The guy was a complete asshole and they hated each other's guts, but their chemistry was explosive. When I got to this *really* hot scene involving the bunk on their tour bus, I couldn't help but notice how this work of fiction so closely resembled my reality. How her boss was the only man capable of lighting her on fire—in and out of the bedroom—like mine did. The only difference was, they got their happily ever after and I didn't.

When I stepped off the plane, I thought I was seeing things. I was so surprised I halted mid-stride, causing a pileup on the gangway behind me. Ronan was standing just outside of the door, eyes anxiously scanning the ramp before they landed on mine.

*What the hell?*

As I made my way up to him, Ronan beckoned me off to the side so we weren't causing a human traffic jam.

"Wha..." I shook my head and tried again. "What are you doing here?"

"I couldn't let you go through with this without giving it one more try."

"Ronan..." I sighed. "How did you even know where to find me?"

He gave me a small smile. "I may have bribed your friend to give up your flight information. I took the one right before yours so I would be here when you arrived."

"Sylvie?"

He shook his head. "No, the other one."

*Damn it, Antonio!*

As irritated as I was with my meddling friend, I couldn't deny the sliver of happiness that had hit me when I'd first seen Ronan. At least until my brain had registered how terrible he looked. He'd visibly lost weight and dark circles were carved beneath his eyes. The sparkle in his baby blues and the self-assuredness that was inherently part of him were nowhere to be found. He seemed... lost, maybe even a little scared, and that made my heart hurt worse than it ever had.

Ronan cleared his throat. "I was hoping the fact that I came all this way would convince you to have coffee with me. We don't even have to talk about what happened if you don't want to. I'd be happy just sitting with you for a little while... hearing your voice. Christ, I just need to be *near* you, Quinn. I miss you so goddamn much."

The tremble at the end of his last sentence was nearly my undoing. Ronan Maxwell could maintain a stony façade better than anyone I had ever met. If he didn't want you to see his emotions, there was *nothing* that could break through his impenetrable wall. Right now, he seemed to be wearing his heart on his sleeve and if I wasn't mistaken, it was just as battered and bruised as mine.

I nodded. "I could do coffee, but I need to grab my luggage before they send it to the land of unclaimed suitcases."

He smiled, but it didn't reach his eyes. "Sounds like a plan. Luggage first, then coffee." He nodded to my carry-on. "May I?"

"Uh, sure. Thanks."

I handed my bag over and started walking toward the baggage claim area. Since this damn airport was practically a city in itself, it took quite a few minutes to get there. As if we both sensed small talk would be useless, we walked in silence as we weaved through the thick crowd of people. At one point, to narrowly avoid crashing into someone, Ronan grabbed my elbow and pulled me into him. My body lit up at his touch and I had to remind myself that things were *not* okay between us. He mumbled an apology after awkwardly relinquishing his hold, and we continued our trek with a few extra inches of space between us.

I pointed to my suitcase. "There it is."

Ronan stepped forward and grabbed my bag off the conveyor belt. "Did you really think I'd miss this thing? You could see it from space." He gave me a full-on smile this time which caused me to reciprocate. The expression felt foreign, almost, but nice.

"It's not that bad," I mumbled, rolling my eyes.

Okay, it *was* that bad. Ronan had given me shit about it every single time we'd traveled together. A few years ago, I had purchased a set of hard-shell fluorescent yellow suitcases. I'd always hated playing the game of, *Is this my bag? Nope!* amongst the sea of black luggage, and this had solved that problem. There was no way you could miss it unless you were completely blind.

Ronan's eyes danced with amusement. "Sure, sweetheart, let's go with that." His eyes widened briefly as he seemed to realize what he'd said, but he appeared to brush it off. "So... coffee?"

"You don't need to grab your suitcase?"

He lifted his carry-on higher on his shoulder. "This is it. I, uh, wasn't expecting to stay long."

"Right." Why would he? I tamped down the

disappointment and pointed to the coffee stand down the way. "That work for you?"

"Sure." He nodded. "Unless... you'd like to go somewhere else. Somewhere outside of the airport?"

He looked so hopeful, but I couldn't let that get to me. This man had *gutted me* and despite how easy it would be to fall back into old routines, I had to protect my heart the best I could.

I bit my lip. "Actually, I think staying here would be better. We could take a seat over by the windows."

Ronan and I ordered our coffees and commandeered a couple of faux leather chairs that were perched beneath an escalator. This was probably one of the least private places we could have this discussion, but I needed that. I didn't trust myself to be alone with this man.

Ronan inhaled a shaky breath. "You're in charge here, Quinn. You tell me what is and is not okay to talk about."

God, I hated this awkwardness. Ronan and I had had our ups and downs over the years, but one thing we *never* were was awkward.

I shrugged. "We might as well get it all out there. Go ahead."

He lifted an eyebrow. "You sure about that?"

*Not at all,* I thought, but I nodded anyway.

He set his cup down and leaned forward, resting

his elbows on his knees. "I can't stand going into work every day, knowing you're not there. Every morning, I'm reminded of how badly I fucked up. Every time a temp quits, I'm reminded of how much of an asshole I really am and how you must've been a saint for putting up with me."

I snorted. "I'm hardly a saint. I imagined doing very violent things to you many, *many* times."

Ronan's lips turned up. "Be that as it may... what really gets me is that *I'm* the reason your career trajectory has taken a nosedive. You're too fucking smart and have too much knowledge of the industry to take this *internship* with Onyx. I can't stand the thought of you working for them—not only for my ego, but because they won't appreciate what they have. You won't be given the opportunities for growth like you would've had before."

I also wouldn't have to see the man who broke my heart every day.

I shook my head. "Ronan, I can't—"

He held his hand up. "Hold on, I'm not done. If you won't come back as my EA, we can transfer you somewhere else. I was serious about that. We can even put you somewhere where you wouldn't have any interactions with me. You tell me where, and I'll make it happen. I know I hurt you and I know you're gun shy because of that, but please, think of this from a business standpoint. If you take this internship, you're taking ten steps backward."

He rubbed a hand over his weary face. "Hell, if you won't come back to Maxwell, I'll write you the best goddamn recommendation letter known to man so you can get something else that will actually challenge you. Something worthy of your skillset. You'll be bored out of your goddamn mind at Onyx, Quinn. You have to know that."

I did know that. I didn't even want the damn job—I'd accepted the position at a particularly weak moment and felt that I had to stick it out. I wasn't going to leave Onyx hanging after I'd already accepted their offer. Plus, I really did feel that a new city would give me a fresh start.

I sighed. "Ronan, you didn't just hurt me. I was *devastated* and... confused. I thought we found something really special in Hawaii and you smashed that to pieces. I don't know if I can ever forgive you for being so callous... for making me feel so foolish."

He winced. "We *did* find something special. Better than any fucking thing in my life. I couldn't possibly regret anything more than I regret my behavior that day."

"I accepted the position with Onyx and I'm going to see it through. I'm sorry, Ronan, but... I just *can't* handle anything else right now." The pure sorrow on his face gave me pause, but I found the strength to stand up and reach for my bag.

Ronan stood with me. "Quinn—"

I shook my head, and lifted myself up on my

toes, placing a soft kiss against his jaw. His sharp intake of breath almost made me cave. "Goodbye, Ronan."

I didn't risk looking back as I made my way outside to hail a cab, but I could feel his eyes on me the entire time.

# CHAPTER TWENTY-FOUR

**RONAN**

It had been exactly four weeks since Quinn had left me standing in a Chicago airport with a gaping hole in my heart. I had come back to L.A., convincing myself that she just needed more time. That she would realize she felt this same level of emptiness—that I was the only person who could fill that void. Any remaining hope that I may have had was squashed when I drove past her house on my way to work this morning. There was a "For Sale" sign posted on her front lawn with a bright blue SOLD sticker.

Quinn's friend, Antonio, was serving as my temporary EA since he was the only person still willing to put up with me. Over the last few weeks, he had been feeding me little bits and pieces about her. I wasn't sure she knew he was doing so, but I would take anything I could get, regardless of how much my ego hated being reduced to this. When I asked him why she was no longer planning to rent out her house—he'd given me that information as well—Antonio said that a buyer offered her well above market value and she couldn't say no.

Since Quinn Montgomery had walked out of my life, I was a wreck. I couldn't eat, I couldn't sleep. The only thing I could somehow manage was work—burying myself in business was the only thing that gave me enough purpose to get out of bed in the morning. I had over a hundred thousand employees relying on me and I refused to let my personal mistakes affect their livelihoods. Although, as the temp agency that blackballed us would tell you, I wasn't the easiest person to get along with these days.

"Are you sure she just doesn't need more time? You haven't heard from her at all?"

I tilted my glass slightly, watching as the cubes of ice slid back and forth, clinking against one another.

"Liam, we've been over this. *No*, I haven't heard from her. She sold her fucking house, man. How does that in any way indicate that she's still in a holding pattern?" I gulped down the remaining amber liquid. "I need to find a way to accept that she's not coming back."

Christ, just admitting that made me want to

crawl into a bottle of scotch and never leave. Hindsight truly was one wise and clever bitch. I hadn't realized until Quinn was gone how much I'd anticipated seeing her every day. Even when we were at our most hostile toward one another, I *craved* her company. Sure, I had wanted to fuck her from the moment I'd laid eyes on her, but I also wanted to talk with her and fight with her, let her steal my food, and watch her brilliant brain in action.

I was so fucking proud of that woman for everything she had accomplished in two short years with the company, and *not once* had I told her that. Not once had I told her how much I appreciated everything she did to make my life easier. Not once had I told her that she was the most important person in my life. Not until it was too late, anyhow.

"Still no word, huh?" Evidently, my sister-in-law had decided to join in the pity party. As Avery lowered herself into a chair on their back deck, she added, "I still think you should call her, Ronan. I don't know Quinn as well as you do, but I know enough to see that she's your perfect match. Speaking from a woman's perspective, I'd bet her lack of communication has more to do with pride than heartache. Let's face it; you Maxwell men can be real miserable bastards sometimes."

Liam raised his drink to her. "Love you too, babe."

She rolled her eyes. "As I was saying... you're not

the easiest lot to put up with. It takes a *strong* woman to deal with you domineering asses. Not to mention your tempers. I get it; it's who you are—it's how you've been so successful, and quite frankly, it can also be hot as hell." Avery paused to wink at her husband. *Lucky son of a bitch.*

"That said, it can also be *exhausting*. You did a number on her, Ronan. I'm sure she's still hurting— quite badly, possibly, and she needs time to recover. But I would also say it's reasonable to believe that she's waiting for you to make the next move. You need to earn her trust back, show her that she's worth the fight. That she's not the only one throwing her heart on the line."

"She asked me to stay away—said if I ever had feelings for her, I'd honor that request. I thought I *was* showing her that I was all-in by doing what she's asked."

"I'm going to let you in on a little secret, Ronan." Avery leaned forward and stage whispered, "We women can be fickle creatures. And sometimes —not always, mind you—but sometimes, we like to be chased. Especially by someone so undeniably alpha."

I groaned and raked my hands through my hair. "Why are women so fucking difficult?"

"Because men can be real fucking morons when it comes to them. Trust me, little bro, I learned that lesson the hard way." Liam laughed. "But do you know what else I learned?"

I raised my eyebrows. "What?"

My brother smiled at his wife with so much goddamn love in his gaze, my chest tightened. "That the *right* woman can make you a better man."

I couldn't stop thinking about what Avery had said. I decided that I *would* make the next move with Quinn, but I figured doing so in person would be the best approach. I promised myself that if she shot me down again, this would be it. I didn't want to cause her any more grief than I already had, but I knew that I would never forgive myself if I didn't give it one last try.

As I was getting ready to leave work, there was a knock on my door.

"Come in."

Mr. Vasquez walked into my office and placed a file in front of me. "Human Resources needs your signature on those to complete Mrs. Chen's job change."

I opened the file and skimmed the paperwork. Li Chen was the senior most person on my finance team below the CFO. When my former executive officer had been arrested, she'd immediately taken the reins as interim CFO. She was a highly intelligent woman who had proved her worth time and again, so promoting her was a no-brainer.

I shoved the file in my laptop bag. "Let them know I'll look these over on my flight and I'll get these back to them as soon as possible."

"Flight?" Mr. Vasquez asked. "I'm sorry, sir, but *what* flight? I wasn't aware you were going anywhere."

"Chicago. My plane leaves in three hours. I'm about to head out."

Mr. Vasquez bounced on his toes and clapped his hands together. "Well, it's about damn time! I thought you'd never get your head out of your ass!" He blanched when I glared at him. "Um... I meant that in the most respectful way possible, sir."

I locked my desk drawers and stood up. "You can make it up to me by giving me her new number."

Mr. Vasquez pulled his phone out of his pocket and furiously ran his thumbs over the screen. "I'm texting you her contact info now. Her home and business addresses are on there as well." He looked up and cringed. "But if she asks, you did *not* get this information from me. I'd prefer my balls stay intact, thank you very much. Knowing Quinn, she'd find a way to castrate me from two thousand miles away."

*No shit.* She was already holding mine in the palm of her hand.

I smirked. "You have my word. Now, I need *your*

word you won't warn her that I'm coming. Or tell Miss O'Hare."

He held his palms up. "My lips are sealed, just as they were when I gave you her flight info. Can I just say one thing before you go? And can you not be my boss when I do?"

I nodded.

"If you fuck this up again, Sylvie and I *will* hunt your ass down and do very painful things. And trust me when I say that bitch is crazy—I'm sure she knows a hundred different ways to hide a body."

I shook my head. Jesus, those two were so ridiculous sometimes, but I couldn't help appreciate how protective they were of Quinn.

"Let's hope it doesn't come to that, Mr. Vasquez. May I leave now?"

"By all means. Go get your girl." He winked and gestured to the door.

I punched the call button for the elevator and listened as the car made its climb to the top floor, stopping occasionally. The doors finally opened, and I was frozen in shock when I saw its sole passenger. She seemed surprised to see me as well because the door started to close again before either one of us could find words.

I stuck my hand in the middle, triggering the sensor to open the doors. I stepped into the elevator, keeping my eyes on Quinn. I advanced upon her and she retreated until her back hit the wall.

We were in the same corner where I'd stuck my hand up her skirt and done very dirty things to her once. If her beaded nipples were any indication, I suspected she'd remembered this too.

Unable to fight this pull between us, I leaned down until my lips were inches from hers. "What are you doing here? I was just coming to see you."

Quinn blinked rapidly. "What do you mean you were just coming to see me?"

I couldn't contain my smile. I knew things were still fucked between us, but I was so damn happy to see her. "I booked a flight to Chicago. I was heading to the airport."

She arched into me. "Why would you do that?"

The elevator started moving. I punched the stop button before it could go any farther.

"Ronan! What the hell are you doing? You can't just stop the elevator."

"Sure I can." I shrugged. "I own the goddamn building. I want to know why you're here and I don't want any interruptions." I moved closer again, this time placing my arms on the bars on each side of her, caging her in. "So, tell me, Quinn. *Why are you here?*"

Her full lips curved into a smile. "Still a bossy ass, I see."

"Always. Now answer the question."

She crossed her arms over her chest. I tried, but it was hard to ignore how the motion pushed her tits up. She had really great tits. "You first," she said. "Why were you on your way to Chicago?"

I looked at her intently, trying my best to convey my sincerity. "To see you. To beg you to move back to California. To somehow convince you to take me back, even though I know I don't deserve your forgiveness. I was hoping you loved me enough to try anyway."

Quinn looked away. "You're right; you don't deserve my forgiveness."

I told myself not to panic just yet. I lifted her chin with my index finger. "But? Please tell me there's a but in there, because I can't stand being without you, and based on how often your friend Sylvie tries to murder me with her eyes, I have a feeling you feel the same."

She laughed. "You're certainly not her favorite person right now."

"Honey, all I care about is whether or not I can be *your* person. If you'll give me another chance." I rested my forehead against hers. "Quinn, I don't want to be without you anymore. Please don't make me be without you anymore. Tell me why you're here."

"Ronan—"

Of course, just then the damn emergency phone rang.

"Goddammit! Hold that thought." I picked up the red receiver. "Yeah?"

"Good afternoon, sir. This is Jim Garrett from security. Is everything okay?"

"Yes, Jim. Everything is fine."

"Great to hear, sir. If you'll give me just a moment, I'll override the system and get you moving again."

"Jim, don't you dare. Listen to me carefully. This is Ronan Maxwell. I believe you know who I am?"

"Uh... yes, of course, sir."

"Good. Now, Jim, I'm having a very important conversation right now—one that I do *not* want interrupted again. Do you understand what I'm saying?"

"You don't want me to move the elevator?"

"Right. I do *not* want you to move the elevator. We are in no danger. I will call you when I am ready to go. If you override the system before then, or call here again, you're fired. We clear?"

"Crystal, sir." Jim hung up without another word.

I turned back to Quinn with a devilish smile. "Now, where were we?"

"You were reminding me how impossible you were to work for." She playfully rolled her chocolate eyes. "Such a bosshole."

I smiled. "You can call me that all you want if you come back to work for me."

Her expression sobered. "Ronan, I won't do that.

That part is non-negotiable." My disappointment must have been obvious because she raised her index finger, indicating there was more she needed to say. "Besides, I already have a job. I just accepted a director of finance position with Coastal Cosmetics."

"I thought you wanted to stay in hospitality?" I said.

She shrugged her shoulders. "I've been doing a lot of thinking since you mentioned finance that day at my house. Quite frankly, I'm surprised I hadn't considered it before then. When I came across this position with Coastal, I knew it was perfect. I want to work for a company that I believe in and they fit the bill. I love their products. They're high quality, eco-friendly, and one-hundred percent cruelty-free. And even better, I get to geek out on numbers all day." We both laughed at her obvious excitement. "Plus... the biggest factor in my decision was that their headquarters are in Los Angeles."

I hated that she wasn't coming back to work here, but I loved that she was moving back to California.

"So, you're moving back?"

Quinn smiled. "Already have. I never did arrange for movers to bring my stuff to Chicago, so all I had were a few suitcases. I think I knew deep down that this would always be my home. There is one slight problem though."

I tilted my head. "What's that?"

"I don't exactly have a place to live. When I put my house up for rent, an investor reached out to me, making me an offer that I couldn't refuse. I have the funds to buy a new place, but until that happens, I'm technically homeless. I don't really want to live out of a hotel because I've been doing that for the past month. I know Sylvie or Antonio would have me in a heartbeat, but—"

"Stay with me." I couldn't get the words out fast enough.

Quinn laughed. "You're not going to even let me finish my sentence?"

I shook my head. "Stay with me, Quinn. For a week, a month, *forever*—however long you want. I have plenty of room and it would give us a chance to make up for lost time."

She raised her eyebrows. "And what makes you think I'd want that?"

I trailed my finger down her arm and circled her wrist. "Why are you here, Quinn? Specifically, *in this building*. Did you come to see your friends?"

She shook her head slowly. "I came to see you, Ronan."

I kissed the inside of her wrist. "Why?"

Her eyelids fluttered closed when I ran my tongue over her pulse point. "Because I don't want to be without you anymore either. But you need to promise me that you will *never* pull something like that again."

Before she could take it back, I brushed my lips against hers. "I love you, Quinn, and I promise, I will do everything in my power to make you happy."

She smiled against my mouth. "I love you, too."

My lips turned up in the corners. "So, what now?"

Quinn's face flushed. "You can start by taking me home so we can have some really hot make-up sex."

I couldn't pick up the phone fast enough. "Jim, take this thing straight to the parking garage. No stops."

"Yes, sir."

I slammed the phone down and took the beautiful woman before me into my arms. "I'm going to screw up sometimes. You know that, right? Not nearly as bad as last time, but I'm going to make mistakes."

She chuckled. "Well, that's pretty much a given. You are *you*, after all."

"But I promise to make up for it with orgasms." I winked as I took her face in my hands. "I was afraid I'd never have you in my arms again. I will spend the rest of my life making sure you never regret giving me another chance."

"Careful now," she teased. "Keep talking like that and people will think you've gone all soft."

I pressed my body into hers, proving how *not* soft I was at the moment. "Sweetheart, that is one thing you will *never* need to worry about."

Quinn laughed. "Ronan?"

"Yeah?"

She looped her arms around my neck. "Shut up and kiss me."

"Yes, ma'am."

## EPILOGUE

QUINN

"Marry me."

My back bowed off the bed as Ronan circled his tongue over my clit. "What?! You can't ask me to marry you when your face is between my legs!"

I could feel his lips curving into a smile against my skin. "Why not?"

"Because..." Oh, God, he was so good at this. "What are we supposed to tell people when they ask how we got engaged?"

His chuckle vibrated through my core, bringing me right to the edge. "We tell them that I was in my second favorite place in the whole world with my favorite person."

My toes curled as he brought me to release. It took me a moment before I was capable of responding. "What's your first favorite place?"

Ronan crawled up my body, lavishing kisses along the way. "I'd rather show you." He demonstrated by taking his cock and lining it up against my entrance. Lowering his head to the crook of my neck, he groaned as he slid inside. "I've been all over the world and there's no better place than right here. I don't care where we are, or if we're living in squalor, as long as I have this tight, wet pussy."

I moaned as he established a rhythm that drove me wild. "Such a romantic." I tried giving him a sarcastic eye roll, but he deepened his thrusts which had me rolling my eyes back for a different reason.

Words were lost on us until we were a limp, sweaty pile of limbs on our bed. I never did wind up buying a new house. Well, not for myself anyway. Ronan and I had gotten a place together right on the beach in Malibu about two months after I'd returned to Los Angeles.

Every morning, he joined me for coffee out on our back deck, watching the waves crash into the shore. Then, we'd head to our respective offices, where both companies were thriving, and come home to each other at night. On the weekends, Ronan took to the surf while I hung out on the beach. I wasn't a strong swimmer, so you'd never see me out there, but I never missed a chance to ogle him in a wetsuit. The first time I ever saw him on a board, riding those waves, I couldn't wait for him to come ashore so he could ride me.

Ronan Maxwell in his element at the office, wearing a designer suit, was a magnificent thing. But nothing compared to the man that I got at home. That Ronan had a surprisingly large collection of band t-shirts and ripped jeans. He laughed freely and loved fiercely. Don't get me wrong; we still bickered often, but I think that would be normal for two strong-willed people such as ourselves. Besides, the make-up sex was hot. I'd never tell him this, but sometimes, I'd intentionally pick a fight with him just to get him all riled up.

"Are you going to answer my question?"

The bed dipped as I rolled over to face this beautiful man. "What question was that? All I heard was a demand."

He grinned as he slowly moved down my body. "Quinn Montgomery, will you do me the honor of becoming my wife?" He took my nipple into his mouth, sucking and nipping until I was a writhing mess. As he peppered kisses along my abdomen, he added, "Will you make my inner caveman happy and allow me to knock you up one day?" He moved even lower still until his face was once again between my thighs. "Will you let me devour this delicious cunt of yours for the rest of our lives?"

I gasped as he gave me one long lick up the center. "Jesus, Ronan, that's even worse! The C-word does not belong in a marriage proposal!"

He blew his hot breath over my sensitive skin

and ran the pad of his thumb over my clit. "Sweet-heart, when are you ever going to learn that I don't follow the rules? I *make* them."

"Such a bosshole," I muttered with a chuckle.

"So, you're going to make me play dirty, is that it?"

Before I could ask him to explain, he sealed his mouth over my lower lips, licking and sucking until I was screaming the same word over and over.

*Yes.*

## ALSO BY LAURA LEE

If you'd like to be one of the first to know about new releases or sales, sign up for Laura's newsletter at:

https://www.subscribepage.com/LauraLeeBooks

# ABOUT THE AUTHOR

Laura Lee is the *USA Today* bestselling author of steamy and sometimes ridiculously funny romance. She won her first writing contest at the ripe old age of nine, earning a trip to the state capital to showcase her manuscript. Thankfully for her, those early works will never see the light of day again!

Laura lives in the Pacific Northwest with her wonderful husband, two beautiful children, and three of the most poorly behaved cats in existence. She likes her fruit smoothies filled with rum, her cupboards stocked with Cadbury's chocolate, and her music turned up loud. When she's not chasing the kids around, writing, or watching HGTV, she's reading anything she can get her hands on. She's a sucker for spicy romances, especially those that can make her laugh!

For more information about the author, check out her website at: www.LauraLeeBooks.com

You can also find her "working" on social media quite frequently.

Facebook: @LauraLeeBooks1
Instagram: @LauraLeeBooks
Twitter: @LauraLeeBooks
Verve Romance: @LauraLeeBooks
Reader's Group: Laura Lee's Lounge
TikTok: @AuthorLauraLee

## ACKNOWLEDGMENTS

**To my husband, Tad:** Your unwavering support means everything to me. I couldn't do this thing called life without you.

**To my beautiful children:** You two are my greatest gift even when you're driving me batty. I love you more than anything.

**To my lovely beta, Crystal:** Thank you for being the first person to read Quinn and Ronan's story. Your feedback was invaluable.

**To all the seriously awesome bloggers in the book world:** Without you, I wouldn't be able to do what I love for a living. Your tireless efforts to spread the love of reading romance does not go unnoticed. I appreciate you more than words can ever say, as a reader and a writer.

**To my incredible Feisty Fae, ARC team, and Loungers:** Thank you for being such awesome, hilarious, wildly inappropriate, and supportive ladies.

**To my editors, Erin Potter of Potter Author Services and Ellie McLove of My Brother's Editor:** Thank you for polishing my work and making the final product so much better! You're both an absolute joy to work with.

**Last but never least, to my readers:** This is my fourteenth published novel and it's been a wild ride to say the least. I couldn't have done any of it without you. It's a privilege bringing stories into your life for a living. I hope you enjoyed Quinn and Ronan's story as much as I enjoyed writing it.

Printed in Great Britain
by Amazon

82597769R00159